Rawhide and Roses

Colorado Dreamin'
Book 1

Maddie James

RAWHIDE & ROSES

A Colorado Dreamin' Book

Maddie James

Rawhide and Roses

She's roses…

Caving to her best friend's crazy ideas is one thing, but Kim Martin knows she isn't equipped for a two-week pack-horse trip into the Colorado mountains—especially with a rough-edged cowboy as their mountain guide. His outdoor style might jump-start some women's libidos, but a city woman like Kim finds him —(almost? barely? definitely?) irresistible.

He's rawhide…

Thad Winchester's patience for city women wears as thin as the seat of his jeans—but there is something about the plucky blonde that puts his hard-and-fast, don't-touch rule, to the test. Kim Martin alternately aggravates and enchants him—but she might just be the woman he needs to share his Flying W. Ranch. If he can get past his rules and make the first move.

When things heat up between them, an argument sends Kim flying away from camp on her horse and into the wilds of the mountains. Alone. Can she navigate her way back to the camp? Will Thad find her? And if so, can they work out this push-pull magnetism between them to some sort of positive scenario?

This opposites attract, contemporary western romance *novel* will leave you wondering if these two characters will ever find a happy medium, not to mention their way permanently into each other's arms.

Chapter One

This all boils down to one thing—*cowboy lust, pure and simple.*

Kim Martin squinted, staring ahead at the string of horses leading up the mountain. She didn't see the pines, or the azure sky, the big white puffy clouds, or the snow-topped Rockies in the background. No, all she saw in front of her was a bunch of horse asses—and cowboys. Which may, or may not, be the same.

"Of all the things I thought I'd be doing this summer," she muttered, "spending two hours staring at a horse's butt certainly wasn't on the list."

She leaned down to pat her mount on the neck, hoping that if she were nice to the old nag, she would be nice to her. She grimaced and cooed, encouraging words to the huge roan mare.

Or were they to herself?

"Just keep your sweet nose in that horse's tail, honey, and everything will be just fine."

"What?"

Kim glanced one horse up to her best friend, Jillie, and

tossed her a fake smile. "Just talking to good ol' Rosie here. We're becoming fast friends."

"Good."

Jillie smiled and turned to face the string of horses. "See, I told you it would be easy," she threw over her shoulder. "They're like robots. Nose-to-tail, down the trail."

Kim made a face. Jillie was an accomplished horsewoman. She'd learned from her father, who exercised thoroughbreds back in Kentucky. Kim didn't know diddly squat about horses. She was more accustomed to betting on thoroughbreds at Keeneland or handing out trophies at the Junior League horse show than sitting on the back of one and riding. How did she get talked into this?

How had they gone from high school teachers to cowgirl wannabes all in one afternoon?

The teacher's conference. The reason they'd come to Colorado. Where they should be right now. But Jillie had this thing for horses, not to mention cowboys....

Kim couldn't care less about any old cowboy. She was a born-and-bred city girl. One used to the finer points in life. And she liked her men the same way. Civilized.

She sucked in a cleansing breath. She'd made it this far. Certainly, the rest couldn't be that bad. Glancing at her watch, she realized the corral was only fifteen minutes behind them. But the ride was two hours long! Two long, insufferable hours on the back of this piece of smelly horseflesh. She sneered at Jillie, who was totally at home on her horse's back.

Kim felt ridiculously out of place.

Her chin length blonde bob fluttered about her face. Risking letting go of the tight grip she had on the reins, she tucked each side behind an ear.

How did I get into this? Bribery, of course. And cowboy lust.

Kim loved Jillie dearly. In short, she'd do just about anything for her. Jillie had whined the entire evening before about a trail ride and Kim? Well, she'd caved.

Big time.

Rosie lifted her head and impatiently shook it back and forth. A burst of adrenaline shot through her. Muffin, Jillie's horse, had picked up a little speed and put several feet between them. Rosie's sonar kicked in and she loped toward Muffin's tail. Kim bounced nervously in the saddle and tightened her grip on the reins as Rosie sped forward.

She wished she hadn't lied about having ridden a horse before.

"Speak of the devil," she mumbled as the cowboy she'd lied to rode closer. Kim hoped he wasn't the one who'd put a hand to her rear, helping her into the saddle as she struggled to get a foothold in the stirrup. She'd nearly sailed over to the other side. Jillie had laughed hysterically. Kim's cheeks grew hot at the memory.

She really hadn't thought it funny.

The cowboy tipped his hat to Jillie, then glanced back at Kim. "Everything all right back here, ladies?"

She eyed him curiously as Jillie struck up conversation. Casual, friendly, familiar banter. Jillie laughed out loud, shaking Kim out of a momentary trance. She studied her friend's face.

Something's fishy here.

"What?" Jillie must have asked her a question, for it seemed she was expecting an answer.

The cowboy chuckled.

"Oh, nothing," her friend returned. "I was just sharing with Mack here your equine-phobia."

Mack?

Kim tightened her grip on Rosie's reins and straightened her back. "Oh, and I suppose you think that's funny?" She risked letting go of the reins for a second while reaching to rub Rosie's neck. See, she wasn't afraid.

Jillie shook her head. "No, not that. He was telling me about a man they had here last week. Tumbled right off his horse and rolled down the mountain a few feet. I told him I hoped that didn't happen to you."

Kim gave her a saccharin-sweet smile. "Thank you very much, but I fail to see the humor."

Mack pulled his mount closer. "Don't worry, I'm watching the back of the trail. Lean forward when we go uphill, lean back in the saddle when we go down. Let Rosie guide you. She knows what to do." He turned away. "Oh, and keep her right behind Muffin and don't let her stop to eat. We lost the last rider who did that."

A wry grin broke his face. Then he glanced back at Jillie, who flashed him a healthy smile. He tipped his hat to Kim before he turned his horse around and started toward the middle of the string. Kim turned her gaze on her so-called friend.

What's going on here?

She kept the thought to herself. "Cute, Jillie. Now everyone will know I'm a novice."

"Honey, everyone knew you were a novice the moment you put your dainty Skecher-clad foot in the stirrup."

"Ha, ha." Kim let her gaze fall from Jillie's face to the pack of horses in front of her. She couldn't help it if she didn't own a pair of riding boots, could she? Her Skechers were as close to sporty as she owned.

"Isn't he cute?" Jillie tossed over her shoulder, her gaze riveted to the cowboy.

"What? Who?"

"Mack."

Mack? *And when did you make this intimate acquaintance, my friend?*

"Oh. Yeah. I guess." For a cowboy. She huffed out an exasperated breath. Cowboys, in her limited experience, were not cute. They were scruffy and dirty and rude and ill-mannered.

"The other one's cute too, don't you think?"

Other one? "Who?" She sounded like an owl.

"You know. Thad Winchester. The cowboy way up there in the front, leading us up into the mountain."

She glanced at the lead horse. Ah, yes. Thad Winchester. The owner of the ranch and their leader extraordinaire. He'd certainly left a lasting impression before they'd started out. Kim found him gruff as an old grizzly. Too business-like. The way he'd shouted instructions before they'd started the trail ride, you'd have thought they were getting ready to head into battle, or something.

"So, what do you think of him?" Jillie asked.

"I don't think about him." *And I'm not impressed.*

"C'mon, Kim, you know what I mean."

Kim rolled her eyes. "I imagine he's about as tough as an old armadillo. Cute doesn't jump into my mind when I look at him."

Jillie ignored her. "Mack says they're good friends. Maybe after the trail ride, the four of us could—"

Kim risked lifting her right hand into the air. "Whoa. You're not doing this to me, Jillie. When we get out of here, I've got a date with a hot bubble bath and a pint of Double Fudge Ripple. You're not setting me up with half of the cowboy-stud-twosome from Durango."

Jillie turned in her saddle. "But they're cowboys, Kim. Honest to God cowboys."

"Forget it."

Kim didn't give two hoots about any old cowboy. She'd take a suit and tie and loafers any day. She liked a man to smell of after-shave, new leather, and squeaky-clean soap. She liked a man to drive a sleek sports car, shiny and smooth, not straddle the back of an animal.

Kim liked polish. Sophistication. A glimmering diamond. Not one in the rough. And preferably one who came bearing roses.

Thad Winchester just didn't fit the bill.

* * *

"Beautiful, isn't it?" Jillie whispered moments later.

"Yeah."

Momentarily, Kim lost her sense of fear. It was a beautiful picture-perfect scene laid out before them. Below was the valley they'd left an hour earlier. Varying hues of green and shades of brown mingled with a kaleidoscope of wildflowers. The baby-blue afternoon sky perfectly framed the picture from above. The mountains climbed majestically on either side. She couldn't deny it was a breathtaking sight. It differed from the Kentucky bluegrass she'd grown up with, which had a beauty all its own. She was almost glad they'd come.

"But I still can't believe you talked me into this. If I get out of here alive, you owe me big time."

"Yeah, well, I'll buy you dinner." Jillie looked at Kim and smiled. Jillie's gaze drifted off as Mack rode up to them.

"Movin' on, ladies," he directed, smiling broadly at Jillie.

"All right." Jillie grinned.

He winked and deftly turned his horse. "Good. Just keep in line as Thad leads us down the mountain." He glanced at Kim. "Remember, lean back in your saddle, ma'am, and let Rosie do the work." He turned his horse and headed toward the middle of the string.

Kim threw him a sarcastic smile, then turned a glare on

Jillie. "Did you freakin' hear that? He just ma'amed me. I've never been called ma'am in my life, except by my students. And I bet I'm not even as old as he is."

Jillie giggled. "Relax, Kim. Out here, I think every woman over twelve is a ma'am. Has nothing to do with age." She glanced ahead. "There they go. I'll get in front, you follow me."

Kim's gaze drifted to Cowboy Thad preparing to lead them down the mountain. There was one thing she could say about him. He was all cowboy with that long-legged, thin-hipped, lean cowboy look. She wondered why Jillie hadn't gone after him. He seemed authentic enough. A chill settled over her, though, as she remembered him glaring when she'd nearly fallen off her horse back at the corral. He was the only one who hadn't laughed and had looked more disgusted than anything.

The man needs to get a grip. Or maybe a life beyond the ranch.

The second Rosie's head lowered to the grass, Kim jerked her attention back to the trail ride. Jillie and her horse headed over the knob—the others already gone before her. Rosie chomped. A tremor of fear rippled through Kim's abdomen. Thad Winchester was forgotten.

Not supposed to let the horse eat.

Panicking, Kim jerked on the reins. The horse didn't budge. "Damn. Damn-damn-damn Rosie. Don't get hungry on me now."

Jillie's head disappeared over the mountainside.

Rosie still chomped.

Kim froze.

"Shit!"

After a moment, she sucked in a breath of courage and pulled on the reins. Hard. Rosie strained against her hands and pulled more grass into her mouth.

"C'mon, honey," Kim sweet-talked. "We've got to get going, sugar. We don't wanna get lost up here."

When her cooing didn't help, she gave one more solid jerk on the reins and Rosie's head came up. Kim pressed her knees slightly into the horse's sides and pulled the reins harder. Rosie started moving—but in reverse!

Panicking at the horse's faulty back-stepping up the mountain, Kim let her hands fall to the saddle horn, just to get a tighter grip. The sudden stopping of the horse's backward movement jarred her for just a second, until the horse moved again—forward, and with a mite more speed than Kim wanted—searching for a tail to put her nose into, she guessed. The panoramic view of the valley below—the one that she had leisurely perused moments earlier—whisked by in a blur as Rosie took off like a shot and galloped over the hill.

"Oh, freakin' hell!"

She was in trouble. Then all rational thought flew out her head.

"Ro-sie... Slow. Down!"

Her brain whirred.

Pull on the reins! Pull! Pull on them!

The words banged around inside her skull as she flew down the Rocky Mountain terrain at what seemed the speed of light.

Pull on the stupid reins? Where in the hell are they?

She risked a glance to her hands wound tight around the saddle horn, the reins woven through her fingers, her ten perfectly manicured fingernails digging into her palms. Painfully. She couldn't move. Rosie descended at a fast clip.

Everything around her seemed contradictory, like silent slow motion and fast-forward, all at once. By now, everyone in the string of horses in front of her had stopped at the sound of her screams. Someone raced up the mountain toward her, shouting. She couldn't tell who or what. She didn't give a damn. All she knew how to do was hold on for dear life and pray she made it to the end of the string. Intact. She felt like flopping fish holding onto a bucking bronco—and knew it wasn't pretty.

And when this thing was through, she was going to kill Jillie Abernathy for bringing her to this godforsaken Colorado backwoods. Even if she was her best friend.

Kim fought back a funny clutching at her throat. Huffing out one thick breath after another, she suddenly felt dizzy, and a little nauseous. She would not make it.

"Lean back in your saddle! And hold on!"

Only—a—few—more—feet.

Good old Rosie. She headed straight for Muffin's tail. Abruptly, the horse met her mark.

Unfortunately, Kim didn't.

In a blur, she rolled over the horse's neck and landed in an unflattering position on her fanny at Rosie's front hooves with a "Humph!"

Hooves?

Or were those boots?

Dazed, Kim shook her head, then looked again.

Boots. Definitely boots.

The toes of a pair of dusty brown boots were the first thing she saw after the clouds subsided and she'd rid her brain of the fuzz. Or most of it, anyway.

Faded denims, slightly worn at the hem, fit tight over the well-worn boots. Her gaze traveling upward found the Wrangler's stretched over firm, muscular thighs. A braided leather belt with a dull silver and turquoise buckle wove through the waistband of his jeans. He wore a denim western-cut shirt with pearl snaps. His hands balled into fists and parked on either hip, his shirt cuffs rolled back to reveal wisps of dark hair on tanned skin.

She gulped. A strange, sinking sensation yanked at the pit of her stomach.

Squinting, Kim brought a hand up to shield her eyes and searched for his face. The sun glared behind him, reflecting off the clear blue of the afternoon. All she saw was a dark shadow framed by a black cowboy hat.

And all she heard was the deep resonance of his voice as it bounced across mountain and valley.

"What in the *hell* did you do to my horse?"

His horse? What did your precious horse do to me?

Kim jumped to her feet.

The last coherent thought she had then, before the bright lights sparked and the blackness claimed her, was that Cowboy Thad seemed a mite upset.

* * *

Thad Winchester knew, as soon as he'd set eyes on the pert blonde trying to get a foothold on old Rosie, this was going to be a long afternoon. He knew it because he and Mack had seen it all before. It was the reason he was about to insist they concentrate only on pack trips from now on. Besides being more profitable, they could insist that experienced riders only sign up for the trips.

Then he wouldn't have to deal with the cute little vacationers who thought it was such a hoot to ogle the cowboys and play Annie Oakley for the afternoon.

He knew he shouldn't be that way. When Mack had suggested they open the ranch for trail rides and pack trips, at first Thad had balked at the idea. He was a rancher. His father had never resorted to other means to make a living. Why should he? But times had changed and today, a rancher had to do what a rancher had to do to keep the wolf from the door. Since he trusted Mack's business sense, he started thinking about it more seriously.

And, since cattle prices were down and the Durango area pulled in a lot of tourist trade these days, well, he'd finally researched the idea and found with a little elbow grease and some planning, they might develop a lucrative business on the side.

But it had turned into more than that. They had turned quite a profit. Thad had become quite the businessman. Mack's experience in the corporate business world had helped. And after three years, he now took his business mighty seriously.

That's why he hated to see inexperienced riders on his horses. And why in the hell they lied to make it appear they had more practice in the saddle than they had, he'd never know. Didn't they realize they were only making things difficult for themselves?

And everyone else.

Like the blonde. He'd heard her tell Mack she used to ride when she was younger. Having your daddy lead you around on a pony twice a year is not the same as having ridden horses. And Mack? Thad was going to have to have another talk with him. As smart and business-savvy that he was, he was also damn gullible when it came to a pretty face.

So, he'd put the cute blonde on Rosie. Rosie was too big for the barely five foot and two-by-nothin' woman and was used to someone who at least knew how to handle the reins.

He'd known there would be trouble from the git-go. And now, here he was, staring down at trouble like she owned the place.

Chapter Two

"**K**im! Wake up!"

Someone shook her shoulder. Jillie? Oh, why didn't she just leave her alone and let her sleep until this nightmare was over?

Kim raised a hand to her face and tried to rub away the cobwebs. Had she passed out for a moment? The last thing she remembered was arcing over Rosie's head like an Olympic gymnast vaulting over a pommel horse.

No, that wasn't the last thing she remembered.

Her eyes fluttered open. A jet black, hooded gaze stared down at her. Simultaneously, her brain and body jerked into alert mode.

Kim jumped to her feet again, angry that she'd let herself in for this kind of humiliation.

"Sit down." Large hands forced her back to the ground. Before she knew it, those hands expertly groped over each of her legs, sliding up and down as if in search of something.

Still a bit disoriented, she kicked back away from him. "What the hell do you think you're doing?"

He caught one ankle to halt her kicking.

"Get away from me!"

He crouched beside her, unfazed. "No broken bones there, that's for sure. What about your arms?" He released her foot. Kim drew both legs underneath her.

"My arms are fine. Stop!" She wasn't hurt and she wanted him gone. Someone in the crowd snickered as the last shred of her dignity stripped away at his manhandling.

"Let me see."

Roughly, he grasped one upper arm and pulled it out straight. His callused hands ran up and down her skin to where her t-shirt sleeve began. Then he inspected the other. "I think you're okay. What about your head?"

"I'm fine." She rubbed her forehead. "Just a little bump." Kim figured she'd passed out more from hyperventilating while speeding down the mountain than the fall. She hadn't hit her head that hard, if at all. She remembered huffing out huge breaths on her quick descent. "It's this damn thin air up here."

"Then what about your backside?"

Heat hit her face. Kim stood and brushed the dust from her backside. "I'm fine. My backside is none of your business. Thank you very much. Now, let's get going."

For the first time during this debacle, they made eye contact. Dark, almost black eyes, narrowed by the sun, glinting back at her like impenetrable steel. Thick dark eyebrows covered those eyes, only adding to the brooding quality he emitted. A thick swipe of whiskers hung over his upper lip. A few streaks of silver graced his temples. His tanned face held a fine, weathered look.

She swallowed. This, indeed, was a cowboy.

"Then get back up on your horse and ride." He stepped away.

"No thanks. I'll lead her down."

Thad jerked back and glared. "Don't think so."

Garnering strength, and realizing she was probably stupid to challenge the man, she grasped Rosie's reins and took a step forward. "You're crazy if you think I'm getting back on that horse."

His gaze narrowed more. He snorted, then grabbed the reins out of her hands. "Get back on that mare and ride. Give me your foot."

Kim narrowed her own eyes. "I will not."

His boots toed her tennis shoes. "Let me put it this way, Miss City Girl. Picture yourself on the gravity side of a thousand pounds of horseflesh and you'll change your mind soon enough. Now get on that horse. I've got a schedule to keep."

Miss City Girl? Why, of all the...?

She had half a notion to hike down the stupid mountain all by herself, to hell with the horses and the riders and the cowboys and even Jillie. Then she thought about what he'd said. She glanced at Rosie, then down the mountain. It *was* a steep decline.

Slowly, she turned to Mr. Thad Winchester.

She so didn't want to do this.

"All. Right. Just keep everyone out of my way. If Rosie starts going like that again, I'm taking her straight to the corral."

Thad brought his right hand to his chin to cover his mouth. Was that a smirk? Then he rubbed it across his mouth as if in contemplation—which only flustered her more. Suddenly, the temperature spiked. Was he *laughing* at her?

Jillie, having dismounted her horse, elbowed Kim. "C'mon, follow me. Get on the horse, okay?" She watched her gaze pass from Thad to Mack and then back to her.

"Fine. Just keep your horse in front of me," she snapped, not too happy with Jillie, either, at this moment.

"All right. Come on."

Kim jerked the reins out of Thad's hands and turned toward

her horse. She stretched to put her left foot in the stirrup. As soon as she made contact, she jumped, then once again felt a heavy hand to her rear. It was almost a slap! This time she whirled her body expertly into the saddle, turned, and riveted her gaze at the man standing beside her. Some chuckles went up from the crowd. She felt the tiny pulsing vein in her neck throb, and the flush of her skin start there and travel upward to her cheeks.

She met his gaze and held. "Don't try that again, mister."

Thad braced his stance and stared back. Not a muscle in his face flinched. "As long as you stay on that horse and ride, I won't."

Horse's ass.

Kim watched him stride to the front of the line, mount a beautiful buckskin, and without a backward glance, start the procession. Gritting her teeth, she clutched the reins, and kept her gaze glued to the back of Thad Winchester's body all the way. She couldn't help it.

She didn't pay one bit of attention to where Rosie had her nose, the rest of the ride.

* * *

Kim threw her leg over Rosie's back, then slid off the horse. Every muscle in her backside was tight, and her inner thighs screamed at each attempt to put her body back into a normal standing position. She stepped closer to Jillie, watching as she smoothed her hand over Muffin's neck and down the coarse hairs around her bridle. She nickered and turned to lead her away, placing a quick kiss on the horse's jowl.

Kim grimaced.

"Guess we need to take Muffin and Rosie to the barn." Jillie turned and looked at Kim.

"I'll take them." Mack stepped up beside her, another broad smile across his face. Kim rolled her eyes as Jillie smiled back.

I need to get out of here. Please, Jillie, let him take the horse.

"All right," Jillie said, her gaze on Mack.

She didn't follow as Jillie and Mack walked the horses toward the barn.

At least Jillie found her cowboy.

The two disappeared into the depths of the barn and Kim stood watching, waiting and ready to get the hell out of Dodge. Thad Winchester strode out of the barn then, halting when he saw her.

She nearly whirled in the opposite direction, but their gazes met and held. Something popped between them. Anger? Probably. She guessed he didn't like to be crossed. Well, the feeling was mutual. But it was more than the precise, narrow-eyed look he'd thrown at her—it was almost like a sensation of crackling tension that filled the air between them. And suddenly, she wasn't sure if it was dislike or anger. It was....

Almost....

Sensual.

Glancing away, Kim stepped backward several quick steps, then bumped into a gate. Turning, she kept her gaze straight ahead as she made her way to the parking lot, wondering why her stomach was trembling.

"No," she whispered. "No. He's a cowboy. He can't make me feel like that."

Shaking away the feeling, she headed for their rental car, trying to rid her head of how he'd looked a moment earlier. She had to forget it. Now. Think about something else. Forget about how his hands felt as they rubbed up and down her arms, her legs. Ignore it. Think about something else. Forget this disaster of an afternoon. It couldn't be over soon enough.

She quickly made her way to the car and grumbled as she

jerked open the car door. Trail-riding was the last thing she ever, *ever*, wanted to do again in this lifetime.

Never, ever again.

Plopping down in the passenger seat, she kicked off her shoes, propped her feet up on the dash, leaned against the window, and closed her eyes.

"And now *she* gets a cowboy," Kim muttered, thinking of Jillie. "Not that *I* want a cowboy, because I don't. *No siree.* Cowboys are rude, obnoxious Neanderthals. Give me a man in a suit any day."

She exhaled. Slowly.

She hated getting yelled at. Hated being embarrassed. Hated arrogance in a man. And more than any of those, she hated feeling inadequate. Why had she let Jillie talk her into this?

Well, thank God it was all over now.

She pinched the bridge of her nose with forefinger and thumb, trying to erase a slight ache starting just behind her eyes. Tension. She needed to get out of here.

Where is *Jillie?*

She glanced out the window and saw Mack toss a goodbye wave to her best friend from across the corral. Jillie waved back, then turned toward the car—smiling. *Smiling!* They were always smiling at each other. It was sickening. Kim clutched her stomach and closed her eyes again, pressing closer to the window.

Asleep. She'd pretend to be asleep. She and Jillie could hash this thing out when they got back to the hotel. She was in no mood for anyone else to take pot-shots at her. Closing her eyes, she tried to relax against the window.

The car shifted as Jillie settled in beside her. Kim didn't acknowledge her presence. The engine roared to life, and they started down the gravel drive. The only thing she could think about at this point was what she was going to do when they got back to the hotel.

A bath. A long, hot bubble bath. Then, a touch-up to her manicure, she'd chipped a nail on her fall. And after that, perhaps room service and a nice long nap. And she'd dream, of course, of men in suits who smelled of spicy cologne. Men who shaved and took baths regularly. Men who brought her champagne and roses.

Roses. Yes. She loved roses.

She smiled.

Not men who reeked of sweat and grime and rawhide.

She felt the car shake as they hit a bump in the road. As they rumbled further down the rutted dirt road, Kim got drowsy. The action of the car's engine, coupled with her exhaustion from the afternoon's events, pulled her into a quick state of unconsciousness. Her last thoughts before she drifted off were of how she never, ever, in her life wanted to see another horse, or cowboy, again—for as long as she lived.

Never.

And then Thad Winchester's handsome face slipped into her mind.

* * *

They stopped with a jolt. Kim opened her eyes and jerked forward to a sitting position. She glanced groggily at Jillie.

"Thank God. I need a bath." She yawned. Dusk was settling around them and she couldn't wait to hit those cool, clean sheets of their hotel room.

Jillie smiled weakly. "Uh, yeah, well, about that...."

Kim closed her eyes again, stretched her arms up over her head and leaned first left, then right, trying to ease the kinks out of her back. She sat back on the seat with a whoosh, then opened her eyes to look at Jillie.

Who was still sitting there, watching her.

She laid a hand on the door latch. "Well, let's go. The further I get away from the memories of the past two hours, the better. I've got plans for tonight." Kim could tell that Jillie heard her, but her gaze tilted somewhat past her out the window. A worried little grin flew over her lips and she finally looked straight at her.

"There's been a change in plans."

"Right," she snorted. "You don't even know my plans."

Jillie shook her head. "Doesn't matter." Her gaze slid out the window again.

Fully awake now and realizing that something was off-kilter, Kim turned toward the view outside her window. She sucked in a huge amount of air, then coughed, her eyes watering." Oh, my God," she whispered, then swiped her eyes with the backs of her hands and looked again.

There was no hotel. There was no Durango.

There was only a large log ranch house that seemed to spread for acres, several barns, and a corral full of horses.

Horses!

Cowboys!

Mack sauntered toward the car.

And behind him was the cowboy of her nightmares. Thad Winchester.

Twisting back, she demanded, "Wait. Are we back at the ranch?"

Jillie pulled in her lower lip and bit. As her eyes grew wider, Kim turned back to the window. Had Jillie just been driving her around while she slept? She could see the main barn down the hill, the one where Mack and Jillie took the horses to earlier.

"I don't believe this. Jillie?"

Silence came from the other side of the car.

"No." Kim shook her head wildly. "No. Tell me this isn't true."

Jillie lifted the latch on her door handle. "Trust me, Kim. It was all on a whim. Well, well, that's Mack over there, isn't it? And isn't that Thad Winchester behind him? I can't believe it," she bantered nervously. "You hush now, okay? Get out of the car, be quiet, and let me do the talking."

Hush now? Oh, as soon as I can wrap my fingers around your neck....

Jillie left Kim sitting alone in the car and slammed the driver's side door.

She yanked her own door latch and fell out of the car toward Jillie. "What in the heck are you talking about?"

"Shush." Jillie threw her a look.

Mack and Thad walked toward them, their faces aimed toward the ground, voices blending in hushed conversation. *Oh, geez! I don't want another encounter with this man.* She slipped behind Jillie's taller frame, hoping the falling dusk would help shield her from view. Maybe she could make herself inconspicuous.

Another couple stood off to their left, carrying backpacks and duffel bags. And there was another guy with a saddle.

Kim risked a quick glance toward the cowboy duo. The only thing she saw was Mack's wide grin shining at Jillie. He chuckled and seemed proud as a peacock. Which made no sense. Her hopes plummeted.

She risked another glimpse to Thad. His nose buried in a clipboard, he wrote something on a small piece of paper clipped to the top. Suddenly, his voice boomed out across the corral and back. He never looked up and still scribbled while he spoke in quick, loud thrusts of his rich voice.

"Thad Winchester, here. This is my ranch, *The Flying W.*

Mack Montgomery, here," he gestured to his left, "is my, um, foreman for the week. What you've signed on for is a two-week pack trip into Starvation Gulch. We leave early in the morning. Everyone will pull their weight. We'll all have jobs. Now, let's see who we got. I don't think everyone is here yet."

He called off a man's name. The guy with the saddle answered. Kim looked about. *What is this? Did he say pack trip? Starvation Gulch?*

He called off another. No response. And another. *Couldn't he just look up?* Then he called out a woman's name. The saddle guy's partner said, "Here!" Next came the name of Thelma Hopkins. Silence. Then Dottie James. That's when Jillie stepped forward. Kim leaned into Jillie's back and tripped a little closer to the men.

What was happening here?

Jillie's words tumbled out. "Mr. Winchester. Thelma is my grandmother. Dottie is hers. They couldn't make it on the trip, and since they'd already paid, they sent us instead. You should have an email to that effect sometime last week. You did, didn't you? Well, at any rate, we're here, and Dottie and Thelma won't be. So, I hope that will be okay, all right?"

Kim's mouth dropped open. *Surely she's joking.* She pinched Jillie's back, refusing to let the word panic enter her mind.

Peeking around Jillie's shoulder, she watched Thad Winchester's gaze lift from the clipboard. He looked at Jillie, narrowed his gaze, then breathed deeply. Slowly, he turned to look at Mack. "What do you know about this?" It was more of an accusation than a question.

Mack shoved his hands into his pockets and kicked at the ground. He nodded. "Thelma Hopkins called and canceled. Guess the email got lost in junk mail or something." He met Thad's gaze head on.

Kim was shaking, but she couldn't approach Jillie with this absurd notion of them going on some pack trip thing unless she gave herself away. If only Thad would leave, then she could talk her out of this ridiculous idea and get Mack to take her back to the hotel. Jillie could do what she wanted.

"Where's your gear?"

Jillie took another half-step toward the men. Kim stumbled again. "Um, gear? Well, you see? Um, Portland, I think. Our luggage got lost on the flight. All we have is we are wearing and what's in our backpacks in the car. Do you think you could help us out there?"

We have backpacks in the car? Kim was so enthralled by Jillie's fabrication that she didn't notice when Thad Winchester took two steps toward them.

"You," he said, pointing at Jillie. "I know you."

Kim hid her face in Jillie's back as he moved closer. She didn't feel the pressure of his fingers on her upper arm until it was too late.

"And you. Ah, hell, Mack. What in blazes is going on here?"

Startled, Kim flung back and faced him head on. For a moment, Thad's dark eyes crinkled at the corners into tiny slits. It was then she broke the silence.

"Don't worry." She tilted her chin up. "I'm not into this any more than you are. Just find someone to take me back to Durango and we'll let the lovebirds ride off into the sunset. I have no desire to make it a foursome."

Thad cocked a thick eyebrow.

Chapter Three

As Thad glared at the blonde standing in front of him, only one word came to mind—trouble—*Trouble with a capital T.* And probably in more ways than one. He'd thought it early this afternoon, he knew it for sure now.

Her glare matched his tit-for-tat. But he also saw something else. Her blue eyes were cool and steady. Although her breathing was labored, she tried hard not to show any signs of weakness, emotion, not to back down.

But the more he stared, he also noticed the little things, like the tiny beads of perspiration popped up in her pretty blond hairline and the nervous quiver of her lower lip. He had a feeling this was a strong woman, one who usually got her way. A woman who was high-maintenance and probably had a good deal of money.

This was a woman of breeding. A woman who sported manicured fingernails, brand name tennis shoes and blue jeans, an expensive haircut, and jewelry.

Like he said. T-r-o-u-b-l-e.

But at this moment, she was a woman out of her element—and she knew it. And she knew he knew it, too. She was uncomfortable, and she wanted out. She was not the type of woman who could make it on a ranch—let along a pack trip into the mountains. Well, he'd see she got her wish. He had a ranch and business to run. He took pride that his trail and pack business was not for the faint of heart. He offered some substance on his trips—rugged territory, primitive camping, and hard work. No time to coddle a city slicker, no matter how attractive that city-slicker might be.

Thad strode away. Pulling Mack to the side, he looked straight into his eyes. "Cancel the trip. Take them all back to Durango." He took two brisk steps toward the ranch house.

Mack matched his strides. "You can't do that."

Throwing him an evasive glance, Thad halted. "Like hell I can't. I'm the boss, remember?"

Mack squinted. "Of course," he tossed out coldly, "But—"

Thad cut him off with a twist of his shoulder. He knew his last comment was out of line. He and Mack had spent a lot of time together on this ranch. Friends since college, Mack had lived with him for a while after Thad's father passed, helping him out. Over the years, they'd always been there for each other.

Even though Mack didn't work for Thad full-time anymore —he ran the family oil business back in San Antonio—he had his own ranch in the valley close to Thad's, and helped work the pack trips as often as he could. Whenever he wanted—or sometimes needed—to get away from the corporate rat race.

Like this week.

He and Mack had never had a boss-employee relationship, and Thad wasn't about to start one now. They were friends. Partners. And that was that.

He dropped the clipboard to his side and looked at the ground. "Look. You know I didn't mean that. I don't think that this woman needs to be here, Mack. She's a disaster waiting to happen. I told you we should have advertised experienced riders only for these trips." His gaze rose to Mack's face.

"Why?" Mack questioned. "You know the trails, and so do the horses. She's a fast learner, she'll be okay. Besides, none of the other ranches take only experienced riders. We're missing out on a lot of business if we don't cater to the beginner."

Thad knew he was right, but it wasn't his style. Surely they didn't have to be like every other pack business, did they? His gaze slid to the two women. Ever since he'd glimpsed the blonde's derriere swinging into the saddle on old Rosie this morning, something caught and held in his chest—something about the woman both intrigued and irritated him.

"I don't know, Mack. She looks a little feisty to me. I'm afraid she'll be nothing but trouble. You know every guest and cowpoke alike has to act like a team and I'm just not sure she's a team player."

Mack shook his head in agreement. "Look. She's had a bad day. Jillie hasn't entirely been honest with her. She tricked her into the trail ride and to be honest, I'm not sure she even knew about the pack trip until now. I wouldn't blame her for being a little feisty. But I have a feeling she can pull her weight, and that she'll come around. The trip might be a good thing for her too, expand her horizons—not that I'm assuming what she needs because I don't know."

Thad listened to Mack's banter and just shook his head.

"Besides," Mack continued, "She's kind of easy on the eyes, don't you think?" He elbowed Thad in the ribs, then shot a glance back to the two women.

Thad cleared his throat. "And if she comes along, so will her friend, whose pants you've been dying to get into all day."

Mack chuckled. "Well, there is that, but what about her? Wouldn't you want to...?"

Thad shook him off. Forget that. He didn't want to admit to

Mack what he'd already noticed himself. The woman *was* easy on the eyes. Too easy. That's what bothered him the most. When he and Mack had started into this business, they'd made one hard-and-fast rule. No hanky-panky with the guests. It was his own code of ethics and one he'd drilled into Mack as well. The city slicker, no matter how feisty or arrogant, no matter how competent she turned out to be on the trail, would be a mighty big temptation.

Mighty big.

She had struck him from the very first moment he'd laid eyes on her.

That was unusual.

And a big problem.

He watched as the two women stepped closer to the car. They appeared to be arguing. "She's out of her element."

"She will adjust."

"I won't take her, Mack. And you will not play tongue-touch with her friend."

Mack eyed him. "Think about this for a minute. Those two women over there represent twenty-eight hundred dollars. *Twenty-eight hundred dollars.* You can't pass that up."

Thad slapped the clipboard against his thigh and stepped back toward the house. Behind him, he heard another vehicle pull next to the corral. Thad turned. Two men, much younger than his forty years, hopped out of the jeep and pulled their gear out of the back.

Taking two steps back to Mack, Thad pulled his hat off his head, tucked the clipboard under his arm, and ran the fingers of his right hand through his hair in defeat. "Who in the hell is that?"

Mack reached for Thad's clipboard. "Aaron Johnson and Tim Rumer, I assume. The rest of the pack trip. A couple of lawyers from Indianapolis." He held the clipboard out to Thad.

"Look at them long and hard, Thad. That's another twenty-eight hundred dollars standing before you. All those people standing over there? You're looking at over ten-thousand dollars for twelve days' work. Ready to throw it to the wind, Mr. Businessman?"

After a moment's hesitation, Thad snatched the clipboard out of Mack's hand, then slowly let his gaze play over the scene before him. The two men had sauntered up to the women. One of them smilingly reached out and shook the blonde's hand. Thad thought he held onto it a mite too long. It only took a moment for him to contemplate the situation.

He told himself it was because the cattle weren't bringing in the money they used to, that there was a leak in the roof on the west bunkhouse that needed fixing, and that his housekeeper, Sarah, kept insisting she needed new appliances in the kitchen. That was the reason he was going to do it. But he knew he was lying to himself. He looked at Mack, then strode toward the crowd, the clipboard slapping against his thigh.

He stopped long enough to turn back to Mack for brief instructions. "Get the women some gear," he barked. "Put them in the east bunkhouse, the men in the west. Tell Sarah we've got six for supper tonight. And make sure we've got a goddamn gentle mare ready for the blonde by morning. Hell, it better be almost dead."

* * *

Kim lifted a worn pair of jeans out of the pile on her bunk. Turning them from side to side, she pitched them into another pile to her right, adding them to the other articles she'd already dismissed: two large, ugly, western cut shirts, a T-shirt, threadbare socks, a belt, a much too large sweatshirt and sweatpants combination, and a rain slicker. A dusty, worn pair of cowboy boots sat at the foot of the bunk.

The duffel bag also held soap, deodorant, shampoo, a toothbrush, and toothpaste.

She tossed her gaze to Jillie, who was trying on the items in her pile, turning around to inspect her backside in the cracked mirror behind the bathroom door.

"He's got to be kidding. Surely they don't intend us to wear these?"

"We're fortunate they have a lost and found." Jillie eyed her through the mirror. After a long pause, she turned to Kim. "You're still mad, aren't you?"

Plopping down on the bunk, she crossed her arms and glared at her friend. Placing the tip of her right index finger under her chin, she looked at the ceiling. "Whatever gave you that idea? The fact that I haven't spoken to you for the past three hours?"

Tucking her fingers in her back pockets, Jillie stepped closer to the bed. "Okay, so what do you want to do?"

"I want to go back to the hotel. You can stay here. All you have to do is tell me the way. I don't have a clue how to get to Durango from here."

Sliding her hands out of the pockets, Jillie sat beside Kim and placed them in her lap. "Kim, I apologize. I was wrong to trick you."

She rose, feeling her face redden. "Oh! So now it all comes out. It was a trick, huh? When did you decide all this, Jillie? And why? Usually, I get some warning about these hair-brained schemes of yours."

But Kim knew the answer to that question. *Mack.* Her roommate broke the gaze and looked away. "I can't explain it, Kim. He's just so...yummy." She looked back and sighed. "I have something to confess. Do you remember the first night we arrived in Colorado? The night you were so exhausted you crashed at eight-thirty? Well, I couldn't sleep. Mountain sickness, I guess. At any rate, I left the room about an hour after you dropped off, just to get some fresh air and take a walk, thinking it would make me sleepy. But I ended up at a little saloon not far down the road from the hotel. It was western and all, you know, kind of like what you'd see in the movies, and the place was hopping. Country music poured out the open doors and cowboys literally dripped out of the place." She paused.

"So, I went in."

Kim groaned and shook her head. "I don't think I want to hear the rest of this."

Jillie grabbed her hands and held onto them. "Yes, you do. I met Mack that night. We danced. Took a walk. Talked a lot. Kissed once or twice. That's all. But we didn't want to let each other go. I don't know whether you'd call it chemistry or love at first sight, but Kim..." Jillie sighed and Kim almost envied her, "there's just something special about that man. I don't want to be away from him."

"But you've only known him a couple of days."

She nodded. The rest of her story tumbled out. "I know, crazy, isn't it? But I saw him again the night before last, and then I finagled you into the trail ride thing. And then, when Mack and I were in the barn putting the horses up, he told me about this pack trip. I guess we were thinking of two entire weeks together. I made up the story about Thelma and Dottie. Mack just confirmed it. At any rate, I guess I wasn't thinking about you and your feelings. I'm sorry. So, if you want to be mad at me for the rest of your life, that's okay. I'll tell you how to get back to Durango, it's easy, but it's over an hour away. I really wish you'd stay. Wouldn't it really be a great thing to go back to school this fall and tell our students what we did? It'll be fun, Kim. Please think about staying."

"That man hates me, you know. He will make my life a living hell."

"No, Kim. He doesn't hate you. You two got off on the wrong foot. Please don't let that stop you."

Kim slowly closed her eyes. She inhaled a shallow breath, then quickly huffed it out. She knew if she opened her eyes she'd see Jillie's pleading face looking back. It wasn't like Jillie's acting on impulse was something new. Kim was used to it. But this thing she had with Mack must be real, or at least needs to be given the chance to be real—and if the tables turned, she knew what Jillie would do for her. She'd do whatever Kim wanted.

Damn it.

She opened her eyes but tried to keep her face devoid of any emotion. "This is the worst thing you've done to me since you filed my picture and resume with that sleazy online dating service."

Jillie stepped closer, and Kim glimpsed a hint of a smile cross her lips. "I know. Sometimes I can't help acting out what comes to me. Forgive me? Come on. This might be a lot of fun."

Kim blew out a breath. "Okay. All right. I'll do it. But I won't let you forget it for the rest of your life and if you two get married, name your first-born kid after me. I don't care if it's a boy or a girl. Got it?" She couldn't help it then. Her face broke into a nervous grin. "And if I die in that godforsaken land out there, you better haul my butt out and give me a decent burial, you understand?"

Jillie smothered her with a hug. "Thank you," she whispered.

Kim pulled back. "But what about all our stuff at the hotel? What about the airline tickets? And I need to call my parents."

Jillie smiled and patted Kim on the shoulders. "Don't worry, it's all taken care of—"

"What do you mean?"

Quickly, Jillie broke for the door. "I called your Mom and told them we'd decided to stay another week or so." She placed her hand on the metal door latch. "And I called the hotel and checked us out. We can cash in the airline tickets easily enough." She turned, opened the door, and put one foot on the threshold.

"But our things?"

"The hotel is going to pack them up and taxi them to the ranch for us. Should be here sometime tomorrow—but too late for us since we're leaving early. Still, we don't need most of that stuff anyway on the pack trip. Oh, and I gave them your credit card number, and told them to add a tip for their efforts."

Great. "But—"

"I'll be back in a little while."

Then she was gone, the old wooden door to the bunkhouse slapping her goodbye against the frame.

Kim fell back flat against the bed in a frustrated heap. "Jillie Abernathy, one of these days...."

She closed her eyes and all she could see was Jillie's bright eyes and animated face. She was happy. Happier than Kim had seen her in a long time. Had she really fallen for this Mack character? That would be a twist—Jillie in love. Well, if that were true, then she had to do this for her, didn't she? She had to play along. It was just that she wasn't looking forward to roughing it for the next two weeks. Not at all.

"You're a softy, Martin," she muttered to herself. "And you're crazy. A fool for people in love. Unfortunately, it never happens to you." She snorted and curled onto her side. All she wanted to do was go to sleep. She didn't want to think about all that now. It was rare that she admitted how much she really wanted a man in her life who would love her unconditionally. In her experience, that man didn't exist. She just hoped Jillie wasn't setting herself up for major heartache.

But someday she would marry, she supposed. It was all her mother talked about. "Find a good husband, Kim," she'd say. "Settle into a nice house in the suburbs on the east side of town. Find someone who can provide for you, make your life easier, give you a sense of respect in the community. Stability. You know how important appearances are, my dear."

Yeah, Kim knew. Her father was a successful local business owner—a bloodline insurance broker. Her mother, bless her heart, had never lifted a finger in her life. She was all for Kim going to college. Thought it was a wonderful place to find a lawyer or a doctor for a husband. But she was disappointed when Kim majored in education—and planned to teach.

The thing was, Kim loved her job. She enjoyed working with teenagers. Before she'd earned her guidance counselor certificate, she'd taught high school Family and Consumer Sciences—mostly food and nutrition classes. She loved to cook and share recipes with others. Food was sort of her love language.

And she was a darn good teacher. It was easy for her to gain the respect of the students, which to her, was half the battle for building a rapport that was essential for a successful school year. She'd start her eighth school year this fall.

Her mother kept nagging her about when she was going to find a husband and stay home and have babies. Why couldn't her mother see that she could do both?

Assuming, of course, that there was a man out there she'd entertain the thought of having babies with.

The men she'd dated filled her mother's expectations explicitly. But they had met none of Kim's needs. There had been no man to spark any kind of lasting fire inside her. And she'd just about giving up finding the one who possessed all the right qualifications.

It was just that all those things, the house on the east side and the perfect man and all—everything her mother epitomized as essential for a successful life—were exactly where she'd always expected she'd end up. But sometimes she wished for something more. Different. Something out of the realm of her secure circle of existence.

Was there more out there? Was there life beyond her Buffy Bluegrass upbringing?

An hour later, as Kim stood looking out the bunkhouse door toward the corral, she watched the moon rise in the night sky, a golden orb set in ebony. The western horizon held a subtle pink glow left from the sun that had slipped beneath it a while earlier. Before long, even that was gone. One by one, the stars above twinkled and popped until they burst through the night with sparkling speed. They did that until the sky was full, like tiny, shimmering sequins against a black satin dress.

No denying the west was beautiful. Kim sighed. Perhaps under different circumstances, if there was someone special to share it with....

Then she saw them on the far side of the corral, and a bitter-sweet silence fell over her as she watched Jillie step closer to Mack, and they embraced in a long and thorough kiss.

Chapter Four

The time was five o'clock in the morning. The sun wasn't up yet. But Kim was awake and dressed in the too-large jeans and someone's western cotton shirt, the sleeves of which hung seven inches past her fingertips and had to be rolled up to her forearms for comfort. The broken-in boots Mack had given her were at least a size too big, so she'd stuffed an extra pair of socks in the toes. Her hair strung down on either side of her face because she didn't have a blow dryer, let alone a curling iron, so she'd just let it hang wet.

And she was staring at two greasy fried eggs, which she would swear were staring back at her.

She hated eggs.

Not a happy camper.

With her hands still in her lap, Kim lifted her gaze to the rest of the party surrounding the large plank table. She and Jillie sat on one side of the table, Aaron Johnson and Tim Rumer on the other. Mack sat at the far end to her left, next to Jillie. And at her right elbow was the high-and-mighty Thad Winchester. The other couple sat toward the end.

Silence ruled the party this morning, a little more subdued

than the rowdiness Aaron and Tim had provoked at the supper table the night before. Of course, she'd not joined in the festivities, she was in no mood for merrymaking, and had excused herself after she'd sufficiently picked over her fajitas, rice, and beans.

It was also difficult not to notice that the only other person half as subdued as Kim, was Thad. The real life of the party, she thought sarcastically. If he had to smile, his face might crack.

He was obviously not a happy camper, either.

She'd hoped for a nice croissant and jam, or perhaps a bagel and cream cheese this morning. A pastry, maybe. Some juice. Even an egg casserole would have been nice. Blueberry muffins. But greasy fried eggs, a choice of equally greasy slices of bacon or slices of fried ham, red-eye gravy, and toast slathered with butter were not her cup of tea—and she would not eat it. How could the rest of them gobble up this wad of grease? Her nutrition teachers in college would cringe at the thought.

In fact, she would welcome a cup of tea. Not this shoe polish they called coffee.

She cleared her throat and looked at Thad. She knew she was about to embark on territory to which there may be no return. But she couldn't help it. What was with her lately? "Ahem. But have any of you ever heard of cholesterol?"

Forks halted in midair. Chewing stopped. And all eyes cast toward Kim.

What's the matter with you all? Haven't you heard anyone speak before?

After a moment, Thad returned his fork to his plate and continued chewing. "Something wrong with your breakfast?"

Kim huffed. "Breakfast? This is a heart attack on a plate. I'm not eating this. And if you all knew what was good for you, you wouldn't either."

Thad's gaze narrowed. "I'll give your regards to the chef," he returned coldly, then turned back to his breakfast in indifference. "Now, eat up."

"Chef?" she chimed. "Any self-respecting chef wouldn't serve up a mess of fat like this. A short-order cook in a greasy spoon, maybe, but no chef."

In mere seconds, Thad pushed his breakfast away from the edge of the table and stood. Kim took in the stone precision of his face—not even Mt. Rushmore compared to the granite statement he aimed at her. Not a muscle in his face jumped. Not one whisker above his lip moved. And his eyes, cold and hard, bit at her with the venom of a rattlesnake. She felt Jillie's fingertips dig into her thigh, likely a futile attempt to keep her under control.

"Miss Martin. I'll have you know that the last time I had my cholesterol checked, it was well below normal and I've been eating this same breakfast for the last thirty-some-odd years of my life. And before you go bad-mouthing the food around here, you might think a bit about where your next meal is coming from, and that it's going to be quite a while before you get it. Around here we eat when it's there, and when it's not, we work. So, if you would rather work than eat, high tail your little fanny out to the barn and start packing up the mules. We've got a lot of work to do before we set out in an hour and I for one don't have time to sit here and argue with a woman who doesn't have the common sense to eat what's put in front of her, the manners to keep her mouth shut, or the decency to realize you don't bite the hand that feeds you. Got it?"

He sat, glaring.

"And another thing, my cook is the only woman in my forty years who has earned my respect and the only woman, besides my mother, of course, who has stayed on this ranch for any length of time. I dare say you would be wise not to poke fun at her cooking. Sarah's not a servant, she's damned near a member of my family, so keep your comments to yourself like a proper young lady should, or you may find your own self slinging the hash for the next few days. Somehow, I don't think you'd fare so well."

Kim eyed him throughout the torrent. With each sentence, she watched his eyes narrow to tiny slits and felt hers doing the same. Where was this anger coming from? Was it just her, or was there something else? Underneath the table, her hands clenched and unclenched into fists, more to help her ease the tension building within than anything. She batted Jillie's hand away. At that very moment, she hated Thad Winchester with a passion.

"Is that a threat or a promise?" Her chin titled.

"That's a promise, honey."

Honey?

Kim glanced down at her plate of eggs. Slowly, she picked up her fork, stabbed the center of a sunny side up yolk, and watched the yellow ooze out of it. She cut a thick chunk, then scooped it up on the tines, lifting it in the air near his face. The yolk ran down the fork and small blob splattered on the plate and jumped onto the cuff of Thad's shirt. He didn't flinch. Kim shoved it a little closer to his face. She never could pass up a challenge.

"You may have eaten this for the past thirty-some-odd years, Buster, but I guarantee you, you won't make it another thirty."

The granite facade cracked. He exploded up off the table in full force, throwing his arms into the air toward Mack. "That's it!" He stared straight across the table at his friend. "Take her back now. It's not going to work."

"No!" Kim jumped up. The only person more surprised at her actions than she, was Thad. She angled her body toward him, inching closer. For a second, she thought she sniffed a hint of after-shave. She ignored it. "I'm not going back, and you can't make me. You offered a challenge back there a minute ago. Are you afraid I'm not up to it?"

"What are you talking about?" he shot back. "You want to be the cook?"

"Hell, yeah!"

"You'd never last," he chuckled. "You can't call in takeout in the Gulch."

"Wouldn't think of it. Try me, hotshot."

"You're on." With that, he turned on his heel and headed for the door. "Show her the mess gear, Mack. Give her an extra mule. Give her Jethro. He's used to packing the cook's gear. Show her the pantry and how to pack the manties, and make sure she's got what she needs. I expect low-fat, gourmet meals while we're gone. I don't want to worry about my cholesterol for the next thirty years."

Kim stuck out her tongue as he exited the room.

He turned on his heel in the door frame. "Make sure it's done by six. We've got a schedule to keep."

* * *

Someone had already sorted and packed most of the food supplies by the time Mack led Kim into the kitchen. A woman she suspected was Sarah, a robust woman of about sixty years, with graying hair twisted into a bun at her nape and an apron tied loosely at her waist, stood finishing the breakfast dishes. Her back was to them as she entered the kitchen behind Mack. Immediately, she felt a tremor of guilt as she saw the woman. She really didn't have a thing against her, or her cooking. Just this thing about anything connected with Thad Winchester.

Mack stepped up behind Sarah and laid a hand on her shoulder. Startled, the woman turned, her face lighting up. "Mack, you scared the wits out of me." Turning then, she spied

Kim and smiled even broader. "Ah, the new cook! Where are my manners? Come in. Come in." She dried her hands on her apron, waving them toward her.

Taken aback at the hospitality that flowed out of this lady, Kim felt her stomach turn a flip-flop and sink. Sarah could have been the housemother at her sorority house back in Lexington at the University of Kentucky. She oozed genteel southern mannerisms and seemed a bit misplaced here in the west. But she looked perfectly at home in the huge ranch kitchen. Kim felt ill. How could she have been so rude a few minutes earlier? She swallowed. "You heard," she returned softly. "I'm so sorry. I really didn't mean..."

Shooing Mack out of the way, Sarah stepped closer to Kim. "I know you didn't mean it. But you sure got Thaddeas riled." She elbowed Mack in the ribs and giggled. "Haven't seen him that riled in a while, have you, Mack?"

Mack grinned and rubbed his cheek as he glanced from her to Kim. "Can't say that I have, Sarah. Can't say that I have."

Then both burst into laughter.

Kim stood dumbfounded, her eyes wide and her lips parted. "Uh, so you're not mad at me?"

Holding her ample sides, Sarah finally stopped laughing and shook her head at Kim. "Child, no. A body who could muster that much emotion out of that man has got to be a godsend. Sometimes he's too much of an old fuddy-duddy."

Kim looked from Mack to Sarah. "I'm confused."

Sarah reached over and patted her arm. "It's just that Thaddeas takes everything so darned serious. It's got to be his way or no way. Sometimes I wish he'd find a woman who would take that bull by the horns and tame him a little. Bring him down a notch or two. He's got some mighty high standards for himself and expects the same for everyone around him. Except for me, of course. She winked. "I've tanned that boy's hide more times than he cares to remember. I worked for his parents for years."

She turned to Mack as if dismissing her. "Take these boxes out the back door. I'm packing up the meat now. His Highness is probably getting antsy to get on the trail." She fluttered about the kitchen, as well as a woman of her size could flutter. "Miss Kim and I'll see if there's anything else she's gonna need... Heck, I might even give her a few pointers. On the cooking, that is, not Thaddeas—she's gotta figure that one out on her own. I doubt she needs my help." She eyed Kim again and smiled. "No, don't think you need any help at all."

Kim watched Mack heft a box of food on each hip and exit the door without a backward glance. She looked at Sarah, whose twinkling eyes stared back. Then, chuckling to herself, Sarah turned away and started for the pantry.

* * *

From the view he had across the corral to the back of the house, Thad decided Mack must have taken Kim under his wing. Damn. That was all he needed. If both those damn-blasted women turned their charms on Mack, he'd be a goner for sure. One was enough. He hadn't seen Mack act so giddy since... Well, since the debacle with Samantha a few years ago. Broke his heart, until she'd showed up almost a year later with one hell of a surprise—a baby.

He could see already he was going to have to remind Mack of that one hard-and-fast rule. The women were hands off. And he was going to have to watch that Jillie. She had an eye for Mack if he ever saw one.

Hands off. He'd do well to remind himself of that fact. The thing was, if he ever laid hands on Kim Martin, it would probably be to strangle her, though he could be sorely tempted to do more than that. Even if Kim were trouble, she was obviously a desirable woman—and one he wouldn't allow himself to break his code of ethics for.

He had a business to run, money to make. And romance was not on the agenda. But had the circumstances of their meeting been different, he might welcome getting to know the gutsy blonde better.

Turning, he finished tightening the cinch on his horse and gave her a pat on her rump. He checked the saddlebags for the provisions for the day: lunch and a canteen, sunscreen and binoculars, and a rain slicker. Slowly, he turned back to the scene to his left. Mack had spread two large canvas manties out over the ground, showing Kim how to put the boxes of food in the proper places to balance the loads. As Thad walked up the row of mules already packed and ready to go, he checked the load of each to make sure they were secure, but kept a precarious eye on Kim as he drew closer.

The denim jeans she wore did little for her figure, but as she bent over helping Mack reposition a box of meat, he stared at her from underneath his dipped hat. She had tucked the old shirt she wore—one somebody left behind a few years back—deep into the too big jeans and had cinched in the waist, showing off her hour-glass figure. As she moved across the manty, picking up and placing items, Thad felt a slow warmth begin in his abdomen. The heat of desire. Recognizable, but unwelcome—and an all too unfamiliar feeling. Quickly, he turned away, back to the mule carrying their personal equipment. He rechecked the cinch of the decker and shook away the slow, easy warmth that begged to penetrate his vulnerability. He wouldn't let it.

But slowly, his gaze wandered back to her. Mack was gone, leaving her to finish the packing on her own.

As Thad worked his way to the last of the mules and horses,

he edged closer to the manty Kim was packing. He watched while she feigned ignorance to his presence, until at last, when she reached for a box of baked goods to set on top of the load, he crouched and grasped her wrist.

* * *

Kim snickered to herself as she felt Thad's presence grow closer. She'd felt the shivers crawling up her back as she sensed his gaze on her from afar, but she'd be damned if she'd let him know that.

When his fingers encircled her wrist, she jumped. Her thoughts were full of him, but she'd had no idea he was so close until his skin seared hers and her senses leaped at his warm closeness.

Her eyes darted upward as she hunkered over the packed items. His fingers tightened around her wrist. Their gazes met. When she looked at him, Kim saw a dark and brooding man, a handsome man, but one who would be so much more attractive, if he'd only let the granite exterior melt away occasionally. His cool eyes still held hers. Several long seconds passed before he spoke.

He released her hand, pulling back as if something had stung him.

"Find everything you need?" he queried gruffly.

Her gaze matching his, Kim lifted her chin and cocked her head to one side. "Yes, sir."

"Good." Placing his hands on his knees, he rose, towering above her. Kim simply kept her position and let her gaze lift upward to play over his face. "I want to be on the trail in ten minutes. Make sure you're ready."

"I'll be ready." She broke the connection and rose, glancing off toward the pack string. Nearby, Jillie worked with her horse, and Mack and the wranglers checked over the packs.

"I want to apologize for yelling at you earlier."

His words brought her attention back to him. She shook her head, surprised at his apology. "No. I was out of line. I should be the one to apologize." She *was* sorry. It wasn't her style to make scenes, usually. "I already apologized to Sarah."

He studied her. To say she felt uncomfortable with the intensity of his gaze would be an understatement. It was difficult to read his expression. A shiver crept over her. "Perhaps we both were out of line," she added.

"Perhaps."

A horse nickered. Kim rotated toward the sound. Out of the corner of her eye, she saw Thad turn and walk toward the others.

She turned back to her work, absent-mindedly finishing placing the objects to be mantied, waiting for Mack to come back to tie them for her and help get them on Jethro. Not thinking about what she was doing. What she was thinking about was the heat that still burned her wrist where Thad's fingers had left their brand seconds earlier. Finally, when she couldn't stand it any longer, she let her gaze slide back to the thin-hipped cowboy who had wreaked havoc over the last eighteen hours of her life. She watched as he swung his body up, over, and into the saddle of the buckskin at the front of the pack. Suddenly, she felt lightheaded and realized she'd been holding her breath. When she let it out in one quick whoosh, all the other sensations she'd been holding on to let loose with it.

Her body gave in to one quick tremor. "Damn."

She moved away from the manties and toward the kitchen, fighting off the urge to pace back and forth nervously. "Damn, damn, damn," she muttered. "I will not let my body respond to that man. I will not!" Her near silent pleadings were heard by no one, save herself, though. "I won't. I won't. I won't. I will not be suckered in by the smell of leather and saddle soap. I won't!"

But she knew as she looked up to catch one more glimpse of Thad astride his horse that it was going to be one of the hardest things she'd ever had to do. For around him, her body just seemed to jerk to high alert. There was no thinking about it.

The next twelve days were going to be pure hell. And not the kind of hell she'd originally thought.

Chapter Five

Two hours later, Kim plodded along on an old gray mare named Sunshine, situated in the middle of the pack string. So far so good. She and her horse had come to an early understanding. The nag was at least twenty years old and moved like she was seventy. Thad led the string up a slow incline into the mountains and Kim followed obediently behind, many horses back.

Several pack mules, she and Jillie, Tim and Aaron, and the couple she'd not put names to yet, plus the two wranglers named Ben and Luke made up the middle of the pack. Mack brought up the rear. As Kim glanced at the battered chaps, hats, and boots the men wore while sitting tall in their saddles, she fell into a fantasy of her own making... Of the wild, wild west. She fashioned herself Miss Kitty, and another cowboy entered her daydream as Matt Dillon. When he strode closer on his horse so she could see his face, Matt Dillon turned into none other than Thad Winchester.

Shaking away a shiver that crept over her spine, Kim let her gaze rest only on the reality of her situation. She was riding a stupid horse up the side of a huge mountain!

So far, they had encountered the remnants of a beautiful sunrise, a misty fog that lifted as the sun rose over the San Juan Mountains, and a host of dewy, spectacular wildflowers as they headed into the Weminuche Wilderness.

They spoke only in whispers and Kim, for one, welcomed the peace that surrounded her. It was as though they were entering the wilderness with a reverence to its pristine beauty. A calm fell over her. If she needed anything right now, she guessed she needed this. Although she would have never admitted it to anyone, especially Jillie, she admitted it to herself. After the hectic past twenty-four hours, she needed peaceful bliss and a calm scenario surrounding her to bring her back into focus.

She never would have thought it, but she was enjoying this immensely.

Finally, she relaxed in her saddle. Her old gray nag would go nowhere in a hurry, but the entire pack string wasn't in a hurry, either. She wondered if this was their normal clip, or if Thad was deliberately slowing things down for her, thinking she couldn't handle a faster pace. Not that he would extend her any kindness. That would be the last thing she'd expect from the mighty Thaddeas Winchester.

She didn't care. Enjoying the peaceful panoramic view around her was all she cared about for the moment.

Her gaze drifted to the head of the string and landed on Thad. She was far enough away that she couldn't see anything but the rigid line of his back as he sat in the saddle and the shadow his cowboy hat threw over his shoulders. Occasionally, when he turned to check the string of mules behind him, she briefly glimpsed his profile.

She had to wonder about the man. Obviously, he was dedicated to his ranch and his business, but did he have a life outside of that? And what was it about her that clearly irritated him?

"Whoa!"

The shout went up somewhere from behind. Momentarily lost in her daydream, Kim started as the male voice pierced the quiet. Quickly jerking on the horse's reins, she stopped Sunshine before she rear-ended the mule in front of her. Then Kim noticed Mack riding up beside her.

"Kim! Didn't you see the gear trailing out of the manty in front of you?"

"What?"

"The gear. Half of the gear is hanging out on that mule up there—the other half is scattered across the last fifty feet of the trail. You've got to watch for stuff like that."

"What?" Kim repeated. She looked two mules up. The mule in front of Jethro had indeed lost half of one of his manties, and now, the load unbalanced, the decker was sliding to the right. The mule didn't seem to like it very much. With a soft curse, Mack rode ahead and dismounted.

"What do you want me to do?" she called out. Glancing toward the front of the string, she noticed Thad had dismounted, rushing toward them. Tim and Aaron, placed between her and Thad, were turning in their saddles to see what the matter was. Jillie, three animals behind her, had already dismounted and was at her side. The horses seemed antsy.

Kim slid from her saddle. She guessed if they'd had to stop somewhere for an emergency, this was as good a place as any. At least the terrain was fairly flat and wide. There was a grassy area on both sides. In front of the string about a quarter mile up, a narrow trail lead steeply up the side of the mountain.

Thad and Mack untied the manty from the right side of the mule and laid it on the ground. They spread the left manty out in front of them and began repositioning the remaining items repack. Thad lifted his gaze to the women, then stood. Hands on his hips, he eyed Kim and spoke gruffly. "On a pack trip, we keep our eyes open, ladies. This isn't a Sunday picnic. We've all got to pull our weight. Lucky for you," he said, pinning Kim with glare, "Mack noticed the slipping manty before we'd started up that narrow trail. We could have lost everything."

"Jillie noticed it before I did, Thad," Mack added. He stooped to snare a duffel bag laying to their rear.

Well, bully for Jillie. Kim shot her a look.

Thad didn't shift his gaze. "Good! At least one of you is adept at something."

"All right, that's it!" Kim stepped closer. She'd kept her silence way too long. "How do you know whether I'm adept at anything? You've known me less than a day. All you want to do is sit up there on your high-and-mighty throne and toss orders out to the peons. I, for one, am not a peon."

"That's obvious."

Hands on hips, she narrowed her gaze at him. "So, what's that supposed to mean?"

He inched closer and glared down into her face. "It means that you're out of your league here. You can't handle a horse. Obviously, you're not used to getting your fingers dirty. And I'm not sure if I've got enough liability insurance to cover any disaster we might encounter because of you. That's what I mean."

"You certainly had no hesitation about assigning me the cook's duties."

"I have every hesitation, Miss Martin. But I also have a rule. I never back down on my word. I'm simply expecting to pick up the pieces once you're finished."

Kim stared him down, then huffed out a thick breath. "Look, Mr. Winchester, I don't know who you think I am or why you think I'm going to cause you problems, but I assure you I won't. I made a mistake. It won't happen again. I'm a fast learner."

It was all Kim could do to rein in her temper. The nerve of the man. Get her fingers dirty? After a deep breath and a moment longer of glaring into the depths of his ebony eyes, she bent over and picked up a parcel at her feet and thrust it at him. "I really don't like you. You know that?"

"Good. The feeling is mutual. Now. Go back and get the rest of the gear we lost." He stepped away, dismissing her, then shifted his gaze to the others. "We might as well rest the animals. It's going to take a few minutes to repack," he grumbled.

Kim stood dumbfounded beside her horse. Frozen to the spot, she watched him turn away, muscles rippling over his wide back as he and Mack worked to reposition the intact manty on the decker. Why were they always at each other's throats? What was so wrong with her that she always got his dander up?

"C'mon, let's get the stuff that fell out." Jillie nudged her shoulder, pulling her out of her trance.

"Here, I'll help. Why don't you stay here with the others?"

Kim looked to her left and noticed Tim Rumer. He offered her a very gentlemanly smile and his elbow. Kim liked the way he looked. Dark hair, cut short. Clean shaven. Smelled of aftershave. His shirt was starched and his blue jeans weren't dusty... yet. He oozed charm and sophistication. A hint of civilization. Why hadn't she noticed before?

Kim smiled, offered him her arm, and glanced at Jillie. "Go play with the cowboys, Jillie. Tim and I will get the stuff. And tell Mr. Winchester not to worry. We'll be back soon enough and then he can get his precious trail ride back on the road, er, trail." She dismissed Jillie with a wave of her hand, then she and Tim took off to the rear of the pack string.

When they were far enough down the trail, Kim reached down to pick up the first aid kit. As she rose, she glanced quickly behind her. Thad Winchester stood apart from the horses, hands on hips, glaring down the trail after them. Quickly, she turned away and hooked her arm even tighter in Tim's. She laughed loud at something he said—she had no earthly idea what—as they moved down the trail toward somebody's duffel bag.

But as her mind registered the lonely, angry look on Thad's face behind them, a heavy thud landed in the pit of her stomach.

* * *

Evidently, Thad decided to ride until they all could ride no longer. Mack protested, as did each of the wranglers, Tim and Aaron, and finally Jillie. Kim kept her mouth shut. She certainly didn't want to rile Thaddeas Winchester any further. It seemed she didn't even have to open her mouth, she annoyed him simply by existing.

They'd eaten lunch in the saddle. Sarah had packed each of them a hearty lunch, which Kim had found in her saddlebag, but it hadn't stayed with her long. Her stomach rumbled incessantly. They had stopped twice for quick latrine stops, but after the first time, Kim had kept in her saddle then, too. She didn't relish the idea of digging a hole and squatting any more than she had to. Especially when it seemed everyone in the camp was hanging around waiting for her to finish. She'd decided she'd wait until they stopped for the night, then sneak off to relieve herself when no one was around to monitor her comings and goings. That is, if she could wait that long. The day long jostle on Sunshine was hell on a full bladder.

When it seemed he'd proven his point, or his anger had finally subsided, she wasn't sure which, Thad signaled to the others and stopped. The wide grassy area sat high in the mountains, a stream running to the left, peaks of the San Juans to the right. Tall grasses willowed with the warm evening breeze and a bird warbled from somewhere in the distance. It was late, the sun low in the sky, and Kim seriously wondered if there would be time to set up camp before nightfall.

Groaning, each rider stretched and eased their tired bodies out of the saddle. Kim stood beside her horse, forcing her legs into a normal standing position, wanting like hell to find a dark shadow behind a huge tree to steal a few minutes of privacy. Instead, she looked around, wondering what the next move was. She had no idea how one went about setting up camp.

She didn't have to wait long. Thad, after barking orders to the wranglers to secure the saddle horses, came straight toward her.

He stared at Kim. "You and Jillie stay here. We'll bring the mules in by twos and drop the manties. Lay them in a row over by that tree and start unpacking." He thrust his arm to the right. "Mack and I will set up the kitchen fly while you find the kitchen equipment. In the meantime, the rest of us will tend to the stock. We'll set up the tents once the stock has been fed and picketed. Once you're set up, we'll expect dinner within the hour. I'm hungry. So are the rest of us. So don't dally."

Kim met his gaze head on and smiled cynically. Quickly, she thrust two fingers of her right hand up to her forehead and flung them forward in mock salute. "Aye aye, captain!" she sang out.

Her gaze didn't waver from his, and she watched as a twinkling of light danced within his dark irises. Suddenly, he seemed all gruff on the exterior, but vulnerable on the inside. Abruptly, he pulled the dark glaze back over his eyes, keeping her stare from penetrating any further. Amazed at the small glimpse of the man inside, Kim felt her throat close and her pulse pick up its cadence. Her sarcastic salute had taken him momentarily off guard and she wondered just what it would take to pull the man entirely out of his brusque shell.

Snapping her gaze away from his face, she shivered and sloughed off that thought. Agitated, she glanced at Jillie and stepped away, almost frantic that she'd even entertained the notion. "Come on. We've got work to do."

Without a backward glance, she pulled Jillie past Thad toward the first two mules, their shoulders brushing. Nervously, her fingers flew over the knots, untying one manty while Jillie held it. Glancing over her shoulder only once, she saw Thad quickly turn away and walk toward Mack. For the next fifteen minutes, she kept her eyes glued to her tasks, tried to quell her jumpy stomach and her pounding pulse; ignoring the pressure of her bladder.

She knew, however, that there would come a time when she couldn't ignore any of those things any longer. She had a sinking feeling that the next few days might prove even more interesting than she originally thought.

* * *

The stream gurgled in front of him. Thad crouched near the water's edge and stared into its depths. Behind him, the horses whinnied now and again. They were eager for their evening meal, too. He should be back there helping Ben and Luke.

But just a moment of solitude, he told himself. Just one minute.

He had to get his head together. He'd acted like an idiot since early this morning. Why, he wasn't sure, but he knew it had a helluva lot to do with Kim Martin.

He wasn't the ladies' man, never had been. Not to say that he hadn't had his share of women, casual or otherwise. And far as he knew, he harbored no weird hang-ups about getting involved in a relationship with any woman, but so far in his life, there'd been no woman to tempt him into anything permanent.

At forty, though, he was feeling his mortality.

Hell, was he having a midlife crisis? Was that why one look at Kim sent him into a hormonal surge? He had felt nothing that strong, that urgent, since he was a teenager.

The pebbles behind him crunched with approaching footsteps. Rising, Thad turned to see Mack.

"The stock is set for the night," Mack offered as he stepped alongside Thad. "Ben and Luke are setting up the dining tent. We can put up the camp stove any minute."

Thad snorted. "Have those two women even managed to find it yet?"

He felt Mack's stare.

"What's with you?"

Thad continued to eyeball the stream. Abruptly, he turned and exhaled. "Hell, if I know, Mack." He sat on a large rock, jerked his hat off his head, and threaded his fingers through his hair.

"You have been a little hard on her. That's not like you."

Thad stopped. "I know that, too."

"Then what is it?"

Facing Mack, he rotated his head from right to left, trying to work the kinks out of his stiff neck and shoulder muscles. He looked Mack straight in the eyes. He opened his mouth once to speak, then closed it again. Finally, he told him, "You know the rules around here, Mack, about mingling with the guests. It's a sound business practice, and I'd advise you to keep that in mind."

He stood.

Mack chuckled. "Are you saying that for my benefit, or yours?"

Thad didn't answer him and started toward camp.

"You're attracted to her, aren't you?"

He stopped and slowly turned back toward his friend.

"Like an ant to honey."

"Then why don't we just forget the trip, send all the others back, and make it just the four of us? No official trip. No problem. We all get to know each other better. What do you say?"

Thad contemplated Mack's words. It was tempting. The thing was, Kim Martin had given him no sign she was the least bit interested. What the hell would she ever want with him? He was no way near her league. "No. Just because I'm attracted, Mack, doesn't mean we can throw the business to the wind. Remember? If there is anything whatsoever that develops between Miss Kim Martin and myself, it will be long after these twelve days are through."

"So, you're just going to act like an ass for the entire trip?"

Narrowing his gaze, Thad studied Mack's face. "If that's what it takes."

He stalked away.

"Well, that certainly won't be difficult," Mack muttered, just barely loud enough for Thad to hear. "And if you continue to be an ass, you won't have to worry about what might happen after the twelve days are up. I'm sure she won't give you a second thought."

Thad watched his friend. "You're probably right."

"Or is that your plan? Push her away and problem solved forever?"

Chapter Six

After unloading four mules, both she and Jillie hoisting eight ninety-pound-plus manties to the side, Kim collapsed against a tree, catching her breath before the next task. Unloading the animals seemed simple enough at first, but she'd never realized how difficult balancing the two packs could be when untying—not to mention the weight of each she and Jillie bore getting them to the ground.

"Come on," Jillie croaked, grasping both of Kim's hands and tugging. "Up and at 'em. We've got to get unpacking."

"Oh, phooey on unpacking." Kim tugged the opposite direction on Jillie's hands. "Sit down a minute. A girl has to rest sometime." She cast a glimpse to the side, watching for Thad out of the corner of her eye, then shifted her gaze to her fingernails, inspecting each for chips. After a second, she glanced around her, searching out a desirable tree for later, when she got to sneak off and take care of her needs. "The slave driver isn't looking. Catch a breath, Jill."

Jillie caught her balance and stood upright. "C'mon, Kim. It's going to be dark soon. I don't want to be setting all this up in the dark. And we've got supper to fix."

"Don't you mean I've got supper to fix? I think His Highness made that perfectly clear."

Jillie waved a hand over her shoulder. "Forget him. If I want to cook, I'll cook."

Kim chuckled and dropped her hands between her knees. "You? Cook? Ha! That will be the day! You are about as adept at cooking as I am at horseback riding."

Again, Jillie grasped her hands and pulled, slowly easing Kim into an upright stance. "Never mind that. I'm helping anyway."

"Ooh, ooh..." Kim winced and grabbed at her backside. "I think I'm in trouble."

"Saddle sore?"

Rubbing her palms over first her derriere and then down both her inner thighs, she nodded. "And how."

"Keep moving. Don't let your muscles get tight. I'll find you something for it later."

"You're sure?"

"Yeah. Just keep moving. Let those muscles get cold on you and you're a goner."

Grimacing as she stepped toward one of the manties, Kim lamented, "Ooh, I think I'm already a goner."

A twig snapped to her right and Kim jumped. Turning, she found herself face to face with Thad.

"You're gonna be a goner if you don't get the gear unloaded and find the kitchen supplies. What have you ladies been doing?"

Kim jumped. She hated being startled like that. Looking into his face, she felt the heat, deep in her belly. She told herself it was anger, that she was so angry with him that the blood boiling just under her skin was simply a product of his arrogance. Suddenly, she felt it had to do with something else entirely.

But she didn't shout at him. Ignoring him altogether, she twisted toward the nearest mantie and began untying it. Laying the ropes to the sides, she was still aware of his presence. By sheer luck, she'd dug into the kitchen pack first.

Thad stepped up next to her. "That's the stove. The dining fly is nearly up. Soon as Mack and I put it up, you can get the grub on." He stepped a few steps back. "And don't waste your time about it. We're all hungry."

Slowly, Kim rotated her gaze to him, her eyes narrowed and her temper on a short fuse. Gritting her teeth, she set her jaw firmly. At her sides, her fists clenched into tight little balls of bone and flesh. She'd had about all she could stand. She was tired, hungry, dirty, and saddle-sore, needed to take a pee, and was not about to take any more of his crap.

She turned a sickening-sweet smile his way. "Look, Mr. Winchester," she returned. Stepping a little closer, she reached out, the index finger of her right hand hitting him square in the chest. His eyes flared as the digit made contact, but Kim acted as though she hadn't noticed. In fact, she stepped another half-step closer. "I agreed to be the cook on this gravy train and that's what I'll do. I thank you not to keep reminding me of that fact because I guarantee you I haven't forgotten it for one minute. So, if you would get your long-legged, arrogant self out of my way, I'll dig into the gear, hoist this stove over to whatever damn place you want, and then I'll start cooking. But until then, stay off my back."

Kim prodded his chest with her finger, punctuating each sentence as she spoke. "I'll do my job, Mr. Winchester. I'll pull my load, as you have already instructed. And whether or not you believe I can, I don't care. But I tell you what. By the time I have supper ready, I expect my tent to be up, my gear stowed inside, and my sleeping bag warm and ready and waiting. I've had a long day and I don't feel like waiting around to do it myself. Got it?"

She punched him in the chest one more time. It was high time she started making demands.

His eyes glinted like sparks off steel. His broad jaw set firm, his high cheekbones like chiseled marble, and then a sly grin broke his face.

It was the only part of his body that moved. The next instant, he reached up, swept off his hat, and bowed in front of her in a sweeping motion. "At your service, ma'am," he taunted, mimicking her mock salute of hours earlier. In the next second, he brushed past her and coolly strode toward the other men.

Kim swirled her body toward Jillie, then did a one-eighty to rivet her gaze on his backside. She hated how man looked from the rear. The way his jeans stretched tight across his ass. The way the muscles in his back rippled under his plaid western cut shirt. Yes, she hated what the sight of those things did to her. Her anger took hold a little deeper.

He was the original horse's patootie.

Irritated, she turned back to the task at hand. Damn sure that he would not make a fool of her, she threw herself into her work. Besides, somewhere she'd heard that hard work was an excellent remedy for sexual frustration.

Sexual Frustration?

"Hop to it, Jillie!"

In no time they had untied and separated the contents of the manties, located all the kitchen supplies, and had informed Mack that all they needed to do was set things up. But all Kim could think about the whole time her fingers fumbled over the ropes was why the thought of being sexually frustrated had even entered her mind?

It was true. She'd hadn't dated in a while. Hadn't had what she would call a serious relationship in about a year. And even though she didn't normally dwell on the subject, she suddenly realized it had been quite a while since she'd been, um, sexually unfrustrated.

But Thad Winchester? Surely to goodness her body was playing tricks on her. She'd never in her life ever dreamed, ever imagined herself being attracted to the likes of...of a rancher? A cowboy? A man like Thad Winchester. A man who held no respect for her as a human being? A man who had eyes like the dark depths of a black cup of coffee and skin tanned and etched with life stretched across high cheekbones, a ridged brow, and a firm, square jaw? Lips thin and smooth. A thick mustache over the upper one. Suddenly, she wondered if he kissed her, would it tickle her nose?

Kissed her?

Kim stood and moodily folded the last of the manties, tossing it onto the heap to the side. Why in the world would she wonder what his mustache would feel like if he kissed her? That, clearly, would never happen. She'd make certain of that. Thad Winchester wouldn't even get close enough to even think about kissing her.

Irritated, she looked back to Jillie, who was conversing with Mack. Suddenly impatient with herself, and everything else around her, she stomped over to a pile of gear, picked up a small shovel and a roll of toilet paper, and angrily brushed by the two of them. Her body was sending her all kinds of signals: aching muscles, a growling stomach, her pituitary gland shooting raging hormones through her body, and her bladder screaming that she'd waited entirely too long to empty it.

And now, considering her frustration with herself and her surging libido, she felt it time she handle the one thing that was in her control. Embarrassed or not, she had to do it. Trudging off toward a wooded area, feeling like every single person in the camp had his gaze trained on her, knowing what she was setting out to do, she found herself a large tree several feet into the wooded area, feeling disgustingly out of her league. And embarrassed.

She started digging a little hole as Thad had instructed them to do before the trip. She glanced around her, never realizing how dark the woods could be near dusk. Quickly, she took care of her business, then headed back to camp, hoping she'd not need to visit the woods again until daybreak.

* * *

Camp was set up by the time she'd finished supper. With Jillie's help, Kim had prepared a supper of meatballs and gravy, mashed potatoes, three-bean salad, coffee, and a small chocolate cake for dessert. Once Mack and Thad had set up the cook stove under the dining fly and left her alone, it wasn't a difficult task.

Mack had lit a fire for her in the stove while suffering Thad's glare. She sensed Thad wanted her to make a mistake, to fumble around with the equipment until she had to ask for help, but Mack obviously was tiring of Thad's manner as much as she. When Thad turned on his heel and left to help set up the rest of the tents, Kim stifled a small grin.

After digging through the food boxes, she'd found a list and instructions from Sarah. Once she'd determined how the packing had been done, along with the menus for the next two weeks, she realized that being cook was going to be a relatively simple task. Sarah had written that the meat on the outside of the box was to be used first, because it would thaw first, and she was to work herself into the middle by the end of the week. Halfway through the trip someone from the ranch would be bring fresh food supplies.

She also found that Sarah had already made the three-bean salad, still chilling in with other refrigerated items next to the meat packed with dry ice. All she had to do was put on the coffee, heat the pre-cooked meatballs and gravy, boil and mash the potatoes, and slice the pre-baked chocolate cake. It didn't take long, and supper was served within forty-five minutes.

Thad made no comment as to her culinary expertise, or the lack of it, throughout the entire meal. He simply ate, then left the party, walking out into the dark night, alone. Kim shook her head to his indifference, then started scraping plates and boiling water for washing the dishes.

Everyone else pitched in. Tim suggested that each should wash their own eating utensils, which they did, and then he hung around to help Kim wash the pots and pans. Mack and Jillie had wandered off to together—she didn't want to know where. The wranglers and Aaron had all gone their separate ways for the night. She welcomed the help, but found Tim a little annoying.

Tired, she appreciated his help and told him so, although it was a little aggravating. She wasn't in the mood to be charming and entertaining. She just wanted to get the dishes washed and go to bed.

She was dead tired, so after they'd secured the equipment as per Mack's instructions and turned on the battery lantern under the dining fly, Kim again told Tim thanks. Feeling like she was giving him the big brush-off at the door of the dome tent Mack had pointed out as hers earlier in the evening, she quickly unzipped the opening, stepped inside, and closed it securely behind her.

In the dark, she could see nothing. Tim's flashlight had lit the way to the tent, but now, it was going to take her eyes a few moments to adjust to the black cavern in front of her.

She sank to her knees and groaned. Never in her life had she been so exhausted. Never. Not even during sorority rush week in college. Not even during the Junior League horse shows. Not even during late nights of grading semester exams.

Having never slept in her clothes before, she found the idea extremely tempting. She didn't feel like fumbling around in the dark for the sweat suit she'd been given and knew that she really didn't even have the energy to search. All she wanted was to snuggle down deep inside her sleeping bag and sleep, oblivious to everything around her, until morning.

It was warm outside, she justified. The sleeping back would ward off any night chills, so she quickly slid her fingers down the placket of her borrowed western shirt and sloughed out of it. The bra came next. Then after unbuckling the too-large belt, she unzipped the jeans, shoved them half-way down her hips, and then realized she hadn't taken off her boots.

"Damn boots," she whispered to herself in the dark. "Too stinkin' big. My feet hurt, by butt hurts, my thighs hurt. Damn old trail ride. Damn Jillie Abernathy," she mumbled angrily. "I'll tan her hide when I get hold of her. Where in the hell is she with that salve, anyway?"

Kim moaned as she squirmed around to sit with her legs in front of her. Fumbling with the boots, she finally removed each, one by one, pulling and tugging until at last, with a grunt, each came off her sweaty feet. A wadded-up sock flew out of one and hit the opposite side of the tent with a pop, then slid to the floor.

"Geez. Now I'll have to find *that* in the morning."

Finally, she removed her jeans, left her panties on, and crawled around on hands and knees trying to find the sleeping bag. Within a few seconds, she touched the edge of the thing.

"Well, I'll be," she exclaimed. "He unrolled it for me and everything. I guess something finally sank into that thick, stupid skull of his."

Kim let her fingers work over the zippered edge, making her way to the top. Finding it upzipped, she grasped the bag about halfway down, breathed a long sigh of relief, and flipped the top toward the wall.

Nearly falling into it, she expected her flesh to meet with warm flannel. But that wasn't exactly the case. Her flesh met with warmth, all right. Warm, hairy flesh. Her body shivered at the heat that flesh radiated to hers.

"My skull isn't the only thing that's thick. And if you don't move damn quickly, I can't be responsible for my actions."

Kim started to scream and jumped back. A firm hand clasped over her mouth before she could eek out much of a scream. Another hand dragged her back down against him, a hairy arm encircling her waist, grazing her nipples as he grabbed her, sending tentacles of anticipation through her body.

She was trapped against hot male flesh, which smelled slightly of perspiration, coffee, and wood smoke. And something spicy. Another tremor passed through her body and ended in the pointed peaks of her nipples, recalling the sensation of his skin against them seconds earlier.

"Don't scream," he whispered into her ear, his voice low and husky. "Or the whole damn camp will come running. I really don't think you want them to find us in this compromising position, do you?"

Anger boiling inside her, Kim silently and wholeheartedly agreed with the familiar voice—then sank her teeth deep into the thick, fleshy meat of Thad's palm.

* * *

How in the hell Kim Martin had ended up in his tent, and his sleeping bag, Thad did not know. But here she was, his arm wrapped around her almost nude body and her teeth sunk deep into the palm of his hand.

He'd woke to the sound of softened voices coming toward

the tent. When he recognized Tim Rumer's mingling with Kim's, he'd cringed inwardly, wondering if Kim had intentions of letting Tim keep her company throughout the night. After all, they had seemed cozy earlier in the day. At that point, a glimmer of something he didn't want to define sliced through him. If he had to put a name to it, he would have called it jealousy, but he would not name it. There was no reason for him to be jealous of Tim Rumer or anyone else.

Kim Martin was off limits. Period.

She'd crept in like a cat and hastily zipped the tent closed behind her. He'd breathed a sigh of relief knowing that he'd have to deal with just her and not the two of them. As he watched her in the dark, Thad let his eyes adjust to the tent's blackness—obviously quicker than hers had—for he had to garner every bit of self-control he could muster to not move a muscle.

His cheeks heated as he watched her hands flutter to her neck and hastily work their way down the front opening of her shirt. His stomach tightened as she jerked it away from her body and tossed it aside. His blood thrummed in his ears when she reached up between her breasts and quickly unclasped the front closure of her bra, allowing her ample mounds of flesh sudden freedom.

Like radar, his gaze zoomed in on the rounded globes. The only thing that broke his concentration of imagining how they would feel in the palm of his hand, was the fact that her own hands had traveled lower to her jeans.

At the familiar ripping sound of the zipper, he'd felt all the blood in the lower half of his body zing to his already swollen groin and had to stifle a moan.

God, how he hated himself at that moment. But as much as he hated himself, for lying there so still, feeling rather voyeuristic, he still imagined his hands snaking inside the front of her jeans, smoothing his palms around her hips and inching denim and lace away from her body very slowly, savoring every sensation of the feel of her rounded buttocks and her soft skin in his hands.

Yes, he knew she would be soft. A woman like her had to be soft.

Damn!

By the time she'd taken off her boots and whooshed her jeans off her body, his blood was boiling in his veins from the sensuality of the moment. Just what in the hell did he think he was doing? If word of this got out, his reputation as a solid businessman would sail away on a Rocky Mountain breeze.

He had to get out of here—and fast!

As her hands patted the tent floor before her, searching for her sleeping bag and mumbling something incoherent, he held his breath and simply watched. She was blocking the entrance to the tent. There was no way out of this. He was going to have to face this dilemma.

Head on.

With her reaching for the zipper and then jerking the sleeping bag open, Thad knew he had no choice but to make his presence known as quickly and as quietly as possible. He sure as hell didn't need the entire camp converging on them at that moment.

The second her flesh met his, and she jumped back, he knew that was exactly what would happen if she screamed. That's why he'd clamped his hand over her mouth and hauled her luscious body back down next to his.

Damn! How he wished he'd at least left his shirt on. How he wished he hadn't touched her, at all. She was just as soft as he'd known she would be. And his hand raking against the underside of her breasts as he held her close and whispered in her ear to be quiet, was nearly his undoing. If he only hadn't made that crack about a certain area of his anatomy being thick, he might have fared better in the whole damn scenario.

Because that's when she'd bit him, and that's when he'd been the one to yelp.

He released her in an instant.

Kim spun away, clambering for her shirt, and quickly jerking it around her upper body. "What the hell are you doing in my tent?" she gasped. "In my sleeping bag?"

Thad let the dark reign silent between reign for a moment. The tension in the air was as dense as the dew he expected on the ground in the morning. Finally, he answered her, choosing his words carefully. "Just doin' as instructed, ma'am."

"What?" Kim's voice flew up an octave at his ridiculous comeback.

"Just gettin' things ready for you as you requested, ma'am," he returned in his most obedient, gentleman-cowboy demeanor.

"What are you talking about?" Kim repeated.

He thought about continuing to goad her, that he was only following her orders from earlier in the day—the thing about warming her tent—but thought better of it. He sat up, rubbing his left palm, and angrily flung the sleeping bag away from him. "Hell. You've got the wrong tent, Ms. Martin. This is my tent."

"What?" she hissed and backed up on her knees toward the other side. "Get out, now!" He watched her arms cross over her chest, and he was sure was trembling.

Hell, he was trembling.

"Believe me," Thad continued, "I never intended sharing my tent with you. Or my sleeping bag. Somehow, I don't think that would be too pleasant for either of us. However, you need to be the one to leave. This is my tent."

"No. Mack told me this was mine."

"Then Mack told you wrong."

"But why would he do that?"

Thad waited a second before answering. "That, Ms. Martin, is exactly what I intend to find out. Now, I'll turn my back while you gather your things and get dressed. Your tent is next to the dining fly. That's where the cook sleeps. Always. Now, if you don't mind, I'd like to get some shut-eye."

Thad did exactly what he said he would do. He couldn't see Kim. Not really. But he turned and could hear her, and in his mind's eye he could see her pulling on her clothing. That image did unsettling things to his libido.

Very unsettling things. Particularly when he could still feel the heat of her skin on the palms of his hands.

She left, and he was thankful for that fact.

Come morning, Mack Montgomery was going to pay. And pay dearly.

Chapter Seven

Kim bolted awake at the sound of her tent flap zipping open. Pouncing to her knees, jerking the sleeping bag up around her, she gasped as she saw someone sneak through the opening. A shaft of moonlight penetrated through the space, illuminating the intruder and the insides of the tent.

"Kim?"

She relaxed. "Jillie. You scared the shit out of me. Get in here."

Jillie entered and let the tent flap slap down. She thrust her arm, and something else, toward her. "Here. Who else did you think would sneak into your tent in the middle of the night?"

Kim took a jar of something out of her hand. "No one," she grumbled. No way in hell she would tell Jillie about Thad invading her tent earlier. And double no way she would tell her she'd been dreaming about him doing incredible things to her body just before Jillie woke her.

"What's this?" She uncapped the jar.

"Salve."

Kim silently blessed her. She'd tossed and turned the last couple of hours, trying to find a comfortable sleeping position. She didn't even want to think about tomorrow. "Thanks."

"Are you really sore?"

She shot a look her way. "What do you think?"

Jillie giggled. "Feels like you've had wicked sex all night and none of the pleasure, right?"

Kim cast a glance aside and dug her fingers in the salve. "Wouldn't know much about that lately and my memory seems to lack in feeling anything like this after sex."

Sidling up next to her on the sleeping bag, Jillie bent closer to her ear and chuckled. "Then you've been doing it all wrong. Making love with the wrong men, Kim. Haven't I told you to drop those wimps?"

"Good God, Jillie." She scooted away. "In the first place, I don't make love with every man I go out with, and in the second place, I wouldn't make love with any man who made me feel like this afterwards."

"Then you're missing out," she shot back. "I bet Thad would make love like a savage. What do you think?"

Her face heated. If Jillie only knew what was going on inside her head a moment ago, she wouldn't have to even guess about it. "I don't think. Now, leave me alone to put this salve on so I can get back to sleep. Do you need this back tonight?"

"Uh, no. I've already used it."

Kim thought as much. She figured Jillie had probably had a little help applying the ointment to boot.

"Uh, Kim? I'm, uh, not going to be, uh, sharing your t—"

"Go," Kim ordered, anticipating her statement, and feigning indifference. She caught a strong whiff of the salve and jerked her head back at the pungent odor. "Go and I don't want to see you until morning. At least one of us ought to have a good time during this nightmare."

Jillie turned toward the door and then hesitated. "Kim, if you're that miserable...."

"I'm not. Just go to Mack. You two are made for each other."

"I really like him."

"Good."

"In fact, I think I'm falling in love with him."

Kim felt her eyes widen as she glanced sharply at her friend. "Already?"

Jillie shrugged. "Well, you know what they say about love at first sight."

Kim glanced away. She didn't want to think about the possibility of Jillie falling in love. "Yeah, yeah, yeah... Well, let's wait to see what happens when you're ready to go back to Kentucky."

The confines of the tent grew silent when Jillie didn't answer. Kim slowly turned toward her friend. "You are going back to Kentucky, aren't you?"

It took at least half a minute for Jillie to answer. "Of course," she replied. "Look, I'll see you in the morning, okay?" Jillie scooted toward the tent opening.

"Fine."

She left and Kim stared into the dark. Something was up, she knew it. And it left a sort of empty longing deep inside her. There was something Jillie didn't want to tell her. Something that was going to change things. Oh, God. She *wasn't* going back to Kentucky.

If that were true, she ought to be happy for Jillie. Would be happy for her. She would miss her, yes, and would stand by her decision, but deep-down niggling fingers of jealousy jabbed at her.

Embarrassed at her self-revelation, Kim plunged two fingers into the salve and massaged a thick glob of the peppery stuff on her thigh, all the while thinking about Jillie's words. If you're that miserable....

Well, the thing was, she wasn't miserable, which was entirely surprising to herself. She was tired of fighting with Thad. Tired of fighting with herself. Tired of wondering if she'd ever feel his arms around her again.

And tired of wondering if she, Kimberly Price Martin, could let herself fall for a man like Thaddeus Winchester? Someone who would love her unconditionally, like Mack already appeared to love Jillie? A man who was bigger than life itself and scared the wits out of her? A man who probably would make love like a savage and leave her muscles sore and wanting for more.

A man who could melt her with one touch of lips, she imagined.

If she wanted.

And that was the million-dollar question, wasn't it? Did she want?

* * *

She woke late. She could tell by the way a miniscule ray of sun slanted through a hole at the top of her tent. It took until early morning before she'd finally fallen asleep. There were certain things occupying her mind that had kept her brain churning and her adrenaline jumping until the wee hours, but when she'd finally fallen, she'd slept like a zombie.

Now, she felt infinitely better than last night. She must have just needed a good night's sleep. But along with feeling better, came a hint of irritability.

It irritated her to no end that she liked Thad's arms wrapped around her. How could she? He was nearly a total stranger! What was wrong with her that she would crave his touch again and again?

She wouldn't think about that now. Now there were other parts of her body which needed immediate attention. Those same parts that woke her from her *sleep-of-the-dead* moments earlier. She needed to pee, again, which was such a damned nuisance. And her stomach was rumbling, which was even a greater headache. Maybe she needed a good breakfast. She'd only eaten a little yesterday.

Grumbling and uttering an occasional expletive, she fumbled around the small tent, trying to find her cleanest, dirty pair of blue jeans and socks. She kept on the T-shirt she'd worn to sleep in, but slipped on a bra underneath.

Dressing without the aid of a mirror and a bathroom, she grumbled some more while she rifled through her duffel bag, searching for that forever elusive roll of toilet paper. Finally finding it, she grabbed the paper, pulled on her boots, unzipped the tent, and stepped out into the crisp morning. Glancing about the entrance, she spied the requisite shovel, and set off behind the tent to a grove of trees to do her personal duty.

Every step of the way, her mutterings grew louder. She was in one heck of a foul mood. Couldn't sleep. Had to pee. Was expected to cook breakfast for a bunch of Cro-Magnon cowboys. Hungrier than she'd ever been in her life. And every muscle in her bootie nagged like a mother-in-law.

She stopped abruptly behind a huge conifer of some sort. It was wide. Big. Had a good deal of shade. Perfect.

She dropped the toilet paper and dug the mandatory hole.

Her fingers fumbled with her belt, then her fly. The zipper lowered. She hitched her jeans down to her hips.

And dreams of Thad Winchester kept invading her sleep all-the-live-long night.

A twig snapped behind her.

She swung around and jerked at her pants.

And Thad stepped out from behind another large conifer. Zipping his fly.

She gasped. Thad turned, hesitated—then a sly smirk spread across his face.

"Mornin'." He tipped his head her way.

"Yeah." *Get the heck out of here.*

After a moment, he walked off. Whistling.

Kim waited until he'd left—and then waited another ten minutes for good measure. Then she took care of business—and left.

By the time she'd returned to her tent, her mood wasn't any better. And if Thad was still grinning and whistling by the time she got to breakfast, she had half a mind to wipe that silly smirk off his face with a spatula.

In her canteen was some fresh water. Had she filled it the night before? She took a healthy drink and then grimaced, reminded that what went in, eventually had to come out. Then stepping behind the tent, she splashed some on her face, brushed her teeth, and tried to make herself halfway presentable. She was getting a little tired of roughing it. It was only the second day. Geez, if she could only take a shower.

Reluctantly, she headed for the dining fly.

* * *

"Mornin'."

Kim rubbed her eyes and tried to focus on the body attached to the voice. The way the sun slanted behind the dining fly cast a shadow that prevented her from seeing who had spoken to her.

"Hi Kim."

Jillie.

Stepping further under, she spotted Jillie and Mack sitting at the camp table while sipping on steaming cups of coffee. She approached and sat down. "I noticed you didn't say *good* morning," she grumbled, glancing at Mack.

"Ah, Kim, cheer up," he returned, a little too enthusiastically. "It's a beautiful morning!"

"Is it?" She glanced around her. "What's so beautiful about it?"

Yawning, she stretched her arms out over the table, laid her head down and closed her eyes. "Got any more of that coffee?"

Someone patted her arm. She guessed it was Jillie. "I'll get you some," her friend answered.

"You better. You are to blame for all this, you know."

"C'mon, Kim. You're having a wonderful time, aren't you?"

Kim opened one eye and arched a brow. "Oh, yeah, Jillie. I'm having a peachy time. This ranks right up there with shopping on Rodeo Drive."

Jillie set the metal coffee cup before her and Kim sat up. "You've never shopped on Rodeo Drive, so how do you know how much fun that would be?"

Kim sipped at the coffee and grimaced. "I just know," she grumbled. She took another sip of the black brew and closed her eyes again. The warmth soaked through her. Her body was slowly coming awake.

"Kim, you've got to cook breakfast, you know."

"I know." She kept her eyes closed and sipped again.

"The wranglers are going to expect something soon."

"I'll get to it in a minute."

"I started the fire an hour ago, Kim, for the coffee," Mack interjected, "but they're going to be hollering soon if they don't smell bacon sizzling. Maybe I'd better to put some more wood on." He stood.

Geez! I can take a hint!

Kim set down her cup. Perhaps a little too hard. Some of it splashed over the side, narrowly missing her hand. "All right, already." She looked Mack straight in the eyes. "So, I'll fix the damn breakfast."

She got up, taking her coffee with her. Mack stoked the fire and added more fuel.

She had just located bacon, potatoes, eggs, and refrigerator biscuits, spread them all out on the preparation table, and was heating a huge iron skillet on the stove when someone came up behind her.

"Why isn't breakfast ready?"

The voice was firm, unmoving, and she didn't have to guess from whom it came. She glanced up from the package of bacon she was fiddling with and huffed out a long breath. She didn't look back. *Please let me get through this without a scene.*

"I'm fixing it."

"It's after six a.m. We should have eaten by now."

She felt Thad's breath on the back of her neck. It was hot, moist. "I overslept," she admitted, still trying to tear into the bacon. She didn't want to tell him why that had happened, that her dreams were interspersed with images of him slipping into her sleeping bag and she'd tossed and turned all night. No, she would calmly fix breakfast, and then get through the rest of the day with as little trouble as possible.

If I can get the damned bacon open.

She reached for the butcher knife sitting by the stove.

"You've got fifteen minutes, Ms. Martin."

She turned, butcher knife in hand, and met Thad's gaze, the knife between them. "Can't you see I'm trying? Why don't you just leave me alone and I'll get the stupid breakfast?"

Reaching out, Thad put his fingers over hers on the knife. "Be careful with that thing."

"I am," she snapped.

"Give it to me."

"I need to get the bacon open."

"I said, give it to me."

Kim watched his eyes. "Take it."

He did, then reached behind her, snatched the pound of bacon, and slit open the package. Slapping both the knife and the bacon down on the prep table, he said, "There."

His gaze penetrated as Kim stood for another second before moving. He didn't move either. Funny, but he didn't seem all that angry with her this morning. He wasn't shouting, his face wasn't red. He was just matter-of-fact stating what he thought needed to be done. Well, if he'd leave her alone long enough, she'd get the bacon in the skillet.

"Thank you. Now, if you'll get out of my way...."

Thad straightened, still eyeing her. "I expect breakfast by five-thirty, *every morning*, Ms. Martin."

"Then I need somebody to wake me up. I don't have an alarm clock, you know, and I'm sure as hell not used to getting up with the chickens. At least not as early as the chickens get up around here."

He leaned closer. "Would you like for me to do that personally?" His voice was low enough for only her to hear. Images of Thad waking her flashed through her mind. But she knew that wasn't what he implied. Was it?

She stepped back, but kept her gaze on his face. "Actually, I wouldn't. I'll manage on my own."

He straightened and backed off. "Then I'll expect to see breakfast earlier tomorrow."

"I imagine you'll get what you'll get."

"What I expect, Kim, is that when a woman takes over a major job like feeding the guests and the crew, she will be up on her own and doing her job like she knows what she's about." He stepped closer. "But then again, you don't know what you're doing, do you?"

She narrowed her gaze. "I am not incompetent, if that is what you are implying."

"I'm simply implying that you are out of your league here."

Kim chuckled. Out of her league? Ha! "Get out of my way, cowboy, and I'll get you the best damn breakfast you've ever had. It might be a little late, but it will be nutritious and satisfying and keep your wranglers happy too. Give me forty-five minutes."

"Fifteen."

"Thirty-five."

"Twenty."

"Thirty."

"You're on!"

Thad glared at her for another second, his eyes twinkling, then gave her a half-grin before he turned on his heel and left. She glanced at Mack and Jillie still sitting at the table, watching. She had to turn away to keep from smiling.

She smiled for several reasons. One, she and Thad had gotten through one entire conversation without raising their voices. Two, he had called her by her first name. And three, at the end of it all, he had given her the most sexy little grin.

But most of all, she was finally going to get one over on the mighty Thad Winchester. Breakfast, and possibly a little crow, was about to be served.

* * *

It took Kim all of thirty minutes to get breakfast out on the prep table, serving buffet style. Actually, a few more, but she didn't think Thad was really counting. She'd had to hustle, scavenging around in the food boxes, and soliciting help from Jillie and Mack. Jillie had fried the bacon nice and crisp, then set it to drain on paper towels. Mack chopped onions and green peppers and sautéed them quickly in a small amount of fat from the bacon. Those were draining on a paper towel, as well.

In the meantime, crumbled a loaf of bread into a large bowl and covered it with a mixture of whisked eggs, salt, paper and a squirt of mustard and a few dashes of Tabasco and Worcestershire sauce. With the onions and peppers drained and the bacon crumbled, she added them to the mixture, along with a couple of handfuls of shredded cheddar cheese, and turned the entire concoction into a large baking pan sprayed with non-stick baking spray.

Then all went into the oven with a prayer that the heat wouldn't be too high or too low and that the whole thing would come out in record time. And she was pushing that thirty-minute deadline to be sure.

While that dish was baking, she started on the hash browns, frying them nice and crisp. Mack made more coffee and Jillie sliced some oranges.

When her time limit was nearly up, she peeked into the oven to see what the casserole was doing and heaved a sigh of relief—nicely browned on the edges, solid in the middle and perfect.

Perfect!

She put the finishing touches on the table just as the wranglers and guests sauntered toward the dining fly. Holding back, she held her breath as one by one they dished up the casserole, the potatoes, and the oranges, filled their cups with coffee, and retreated to the camp tables. Mack and Jillie followed.

Then Thad.

He eyed the table, raking his gaze over what she had prepared. Then he turned, slowly, toward her. Their gazes met and Kim fought off the urge to tremble.

He picked up two plates, extended one to her. "Time to eat," he said, no expression on his face.

Tentatively, she eased forward and took the plate.

"Looks good," he said.

She wanted to smile, resisted. "It is."

Thad's gaze slid toward the guests and wranglers. Not a sound came from the tables except for forks clanking and an occasional slurp. "Nutritious and satisfying all at the same time," he added.

Kim nodded.

"Well then," he turned back to the food. "Let's eat and get on the trail."

He dished up a healthy serving of the casserole. Kim let out a slow, even breath. And smiled.

* * *

Later, she couldn't believe she'd survived the better part of another day riding deeper into the San Juan Mountains. Thad had suggested at breakfast that they would ride until late afternoon, then make camp at an old mining town near Bear Creek that evening. He said they'd camp there for the next several nights, depending, then move on toward Elk Park after that. They'd move east of there until it was time for the guests to catch the Narrow Gauge train back to Durango, then they'd head into Elk Park and catch the spur. Thad, Mack, and the wranglers would return to the ranch with the horses and mules.

The twelve-mile ride on old Sunshine had proven uneventful, allowing her the luxury of perusing vistas as large as the world itself, as well as a moment or two of self-reflection. The scenery about her was too enormous and panoramic to allow many thoughts of Thad to creep into her mind. Well, at least for most of the day. Images of his hands on her body crept upon her one too many times, sending involuntary shivers down her spine, but she shook them off and tried to concentrate on the scenery.

She allowed herself only a few moments of panic as they traveled up and down the narrow and treacherous trails at the top of the world—and at 11,000-plus feet above sea level, that's exactly where Kim felt they were. They'd maneuvered through rocky passes, meadows of small, dazzling wildflowers, and patches of lush forest. As they rose higher, the mountains in the distance became rocky and bare.

Sunshine handled herself nicely and Kim breathed a little easier with each step up the trail. Now, as they neared the old mine camp, she inhaled huge breaths of the thin, crisp, mountain air until she felt dizzy.

A mountain stream, which she assumed was Bear Creek, bordered their camp site. She could hear the waters rushing in the distance and wondered if there might be a waterfall nearby. Suddenly, the sight before her paled all her past problems significantly at the dramatic sense of serenity it brought her. Every muscle in her body relaxed.

In a way, she was glad Jillie had tricked her. Never in her life had she experienced anything so dramatic and memorable, as well as promoting a bit of self-sufficiency at the same time. She only wished she hadn't left her camera back at the hotel. They'd never believe this back home.

Camp was set up routinely, having been through it once before now, and Kim, Jillie, and Tim had supper simmering on the stove within the hour. Much to Jillie's distress and Kim's amazement, Tim seemed to have appointed himself the cook's helper while his buddy Aaron tackled feeding and picketing the livestock with the wranglers. They made jokes and laughed away the minutes as Kim played chef and ordered them about. She hardly had a minute throughout the camaraderie to even think of Thad. Of course, there were seconds his image crept into her thoughts.

Thad had made himself scarce most of the day. It wasn't as though she were keeping tabs on him or anything, well, kind of... but not really, she mused. But it was obvious he was avoiding her.

At breakfast he'd inhaled his food and threw his coffee back so quickly Kim had to wonder how he'd kept from scalding his throat. After she and her so-called cook's crew had cleaned up breakfast and had broken down the kitchen and tent, they'd assisted with the packing and loading of the mules again, but Thad had found things away from her to occupy his time.

Kim watched his back throughout the afternoon as he led them further into the wilderness, and for the first time, she realized she trusted him. She acknowledged that he obviously knew what he was doing and was competent enough not to lead them into dangerous situations.

But each time they stopped, he made it a point to stay near the wranglers. He never ventured near Jillie or herself, or even Mack, Tim, or Aaron. In fact, she'd caught herself staring at him once, while he was laughing and joking with the wranglers, and felt an instant stab of jealousy. Why couldn't he be so at ease around her? Wouldn't it be nice, she thought, if they could get through one day, one meal even, with some trivial banter and camaraderie?

And now, as Kim prepared to dish up the dinner of barbecued chicken, baked potatoes, green beans, and a tossed salad she'd thrown together, she watched for him out of the corner of her eye. He was standoffish, separating himself from the rest of the group. When at last each member of the party but Thad had been served, and Kim was helping herself to portions of the meal, she saw the looming shadow fall over the food in front of her and felt the tiny hairs on the back of her neck stand on end.

She also heard the pounding of her heart and silently prayed for it to stop. She was afraid everyone else in the camp heard it, too.

Slowly, she dished a hefty spoonful of green beans onto her plate and set the spoon back in the pan. Without a thought, she picked up the last plate on the table and turned to hand it to Thad.

His large hand hesitated, then reached out to grasp the plate. Lifting her head to look into his face, their eyes met, and Kim froze. After a moment, she absentmindedly shoved the plate toward him and looked away without another gesture or comment. Dizzily, she turned and stepped away from the stove to join the others.

But the image of his eyes stayed with her, taking hold, and wrapping around her like a warm blanket. Red-rimmed, as if from lack of sleep, his eyes looked tired. But the facade would hold steady, she was sure. He wouldn't admit fatigue if his life depended on it.

And as Kim stepped toward the table filled with cowboys and guests, she had to wonder what kept Thad from sleeping last night. Could it be the same thing that had kept her awake deep into the night?

She shook her head. Thad wouldn't be the type of man to let himself brood over something as silly as a mistake. And the chance meeting of their bodies last night had indeed been that. A mistake.

Unless...there was more to it than that.

She halted as she neared the table, afraid to contemplate the question that bounced about inside her brain and glanced at the group. To her left, she could swear she saw Jillie slide to the edge of the bench across from Mack, taking up space for another person. And there were no other seats available at the table.

She approached Jillie. "Scoot over, Jill," she whispered. "Let me sit by you."

Jillie stopped chewing a bite of salad and glanced to her left, then right. "Umm...there's really not a lot of room here, Kim. Why don't you sit at the picnic table over there?"

Kim's gaze followed the direction of Jillie's pointing finger. An old picnic table, weathered and rotting, left by someone years ago, sat several feet away from the dining fly.

She pulled her gaze back to Jillie. "C'mon, Jillie, that thing's falling apart. Scoot over."

Jillie shook her head. "Go on Kim. I'm a lefty, you know that. I'll elbow you in the ribs the entire meal." She turned her attention to her barbecued chicken, sinking her fork into a piece of juicy thigh meat.

Kim dismissed her with a grumble and glanced quickly at the rest of the group, all eating hungrily. Even Tim didn't seem interested in more than his meal now. Shrugging, she headed for the solitary table.

After a minute or so into her meal, the shadow crossed her plate again.

Thad sat across from her without a sound, or any acknowledgment that he was not the only person at the table. For several minutes, she ate, every once in a while lifting her gaze to snatch a glimpse of him. He kept his attention on his food. Kim noticed he heartily sampled all her dishes and before long, his entire plate was clean. Finally, like a satisfied male, he looked up to catch her watching him. Funny how the notion that she'd satisfied his stomach made her wonder if she could satisfy him in other ways as well.

A thrill burst up through her at that moment and she realized that ever since last night, ever since she'd felt Thad's hard, warm arms wrapped around her naked torso, her brain and her hormones had been thinking the same thing. Could she satisfy a man like Thad Winchester? Correction. Not a man like Thad Winchester, but Thad himself?

Those cool, dark eyes bore into hers and a white-hot shiver raced across her shoulders. "So..." she interjected, glancing toward his plate, "ready for seconds?"

Shit! Seconds? Her brain went to last night.

Hesitating, Thad shook his head. "No," he finally answered. "Thank you, though," he added.

"Oh. That bad, huh?" Her gaze kept pace with his, her pulse kept rhythm with...something.

A glimmer raced through his eyes. "No. The supper was adequate. You've handled yourself quite well in the kitchen."

Was that statement an actual compliment? "It's second nature."

"Oh?"

She watched the thin line of brow running over his eyes arch in animation and his jaw grow slack. She was more used to the narrowed, hooded expression he usually sported, but suddenly found his face quite attractive since he'd momentarily rid it of the scowl. Not that she hadn't found him attractive before, that is, if one went after the rugged look, which she didn't, usually, but....

Kim leaned both elbows over the table and drew closer to Thad. She squinted against the setting sun and felt one corner of her mouth draw up into what might be described as a smirk. Discussion of the dinner was more easily handled now than the thought of her and Thad together. And for once, they weren't yelling at each other. "That meal was more than *adequate* and you know it, Thad Winchester," she threw out playfully.

Am I flirting?

Echoing her lean, Thad's face inched closer. "Well, I might be willing to up the rating to satisfactory if I had some desert and coffee."

Is he flirting?

"Regular or decaf?" They both knew there was nothing but regular.

Thad pulled himself back at the quick comeback and Kim saw a hint of a grin pass over his lips. "Regular. I sleep like a log. What's for dessert?"

"Pound cake with strawberries. And you didn't sleep like a log last night. Cream or sugar?" She drew in over the space of the table again, becoming accustomed to this strange banter between them.

"Black. And no strawberries. I'm allergic. Why don't you think I slept well?"

She rose, her gaze holding his steady, picked up her plate, and reached across the table for his. "Because I didn't, either."

Thad's fingers wrapped around her wrist, stopping her, and her gaze shot to his hand. An ever-so-gentle tug pulled her slightly closer. Kim felt drawn to him. The tug likely wasn't necessary. The physical pulling of her closer wouldn't have mattered at all. Her plate fell to the ground with a clank and rattle. She had practically stopped breathing the instant his hot fingers curled around her wrist.

But when she brought her gaze back to his face, it was like carved marble. "I can do that myself," he said. "You don't have to wait on me." His eyes were glinted steel and full of warning. Warning of what, she just wasn't sure.

Not to cross him? Or get too close?

"It's not my nature to wait on anyone, Thad, unless I choose to. Now, if you'll kindly unhand me, I'll get us both some cake and coffee."

He did, and she picked up her plate, stepping away from the rickety old picnic table that held the larger-than-life male behind her. An erratic tattoo beat against her chest and her brain registered the fact that she needed to breathe.

What the hell was wrong with her? Could it be that Thad Winchester did more to her than just kick her hormones into full gear? Could it be that those fleeting, vulnerable and irresistible looks he gave her were getting to her?

"And why am I bringing him cake and coffee?" Why did she even *want* to do that? She was more used to men bringing things *to her*, rather than the other way around.

She *wanted* him. That was why. She wanted him badly.

With every molecule of her being. She wanted him unlike any man she'd ever wanted before. And admitting that only fanned the flames more. But even at that, she knew it would be a cold day in hell before he would entertain any notion of wanting her. Especially for anything other than a quick romp in a sleeping bag. There was nothing permanent about what Thad could offer her. He was not the man she needed.

And she wasn't up for a vacation romance. Obviously, that would be all they'd ever have. Picturing Thad in her world was ridiculous. Picturing herself in his was...was, well, just....

As ridiculous.

Well, no matter. She would not be a party to the whims of Thad Winchester, no matter how inviting. She had to control those raging hormones inside of her, tamp them down and settle them all prim and proper and ladylike. She wouldn't settle for anyone who didn't scream permanent relationship. Or at least long-term. Very long-term. Thad was a quickie waiting to happen, and she was as ripe as an August tomato.

She couldn't fall under that rugged spell of testosterone. She couldn't allow herself to be drawn into his sexy web of maleness. She'd been tricked into a two-week pack trip that wasn't nearly as bad as she'd originally thought—in fact was enjoying, to a point—and then she was going home. To Kentucky. To her students. The career she'd worked so hard for. And to the real world.

It all boiled down to one thing: *I have to stay away from Thad Winchester.* The smell of rawhide was just too darn appealing these days.

Absentmindedly, Kim looked down and tossed the dirty dishes into an empty dish pan, glanced once at the coffeepot and pound cake, then turned on her heel and headed for the privacy of her tent.

Forget dessert. Of any kind.

Chapter Eight

Across the leaping circle of orange and red flames, Thad sat alone and stared into the fire. He had intentionally separated himself from the group. There had been marshmallows to roast on thin branches, and lively conversation from the guests and his men, but he hadn't gotten involved. He couldn't let his guard down long enough tonight to allow himself camaraderie. He was afraid he'd slip, drift over to Kim's side, and before he realized it, pull her close to him. It was an image that kept creeping into his mind; he had to get rid of it.

It was extremely important that he keep his guard up for the remainder of the trip. It would be all too easy for him to let it down to a point where he'd never get it back up again.

He wasn't up for that risk. He had to set the example for his men. Hadn't he just fired one of his best wranglers less than two weeks ago because he'd sneaked off with a guest for a little afternoon delight? Yes, he had. And Ben and Luke would be watching, not that they were deliberately trying to catch him at anything. They were good men, and loyal, and he wanted to keep it that way. And Mack, he was going to have to keep his distance from Jillie, or...well, he didn't want to think about the outcome.

He turned his attention to his guests. The two city-slickers from Indiana had made themselves quite at home. One fancied himself a cowboy and hung close to the wranglers, and the other liked to fancy himself the dandy. But every time he inched closer to Kim, Thad felt his gut tighten.

He was jealous of the freedom to flirt, to get close to her. Perhaps after the pack trip....

Naw. There wouldn't be time. She'd return to wherever it was she'd come from, and he would never see her again. He just had to face it, no matter how attracted he was to the woman, as long as she was involved in the pack trip and he was the proprietor of that trip, there'd be no chance in hell that they would ever get together.

But perhaps, just perhaps when all this was through, if he could get an email address, a phone number....

His gaze shifted. Heat from the fire flared before him, rivaling only the desire boiling up inside his gut much like the red embers roiling in front of him.

Watching her toss her short, blonde hair back as she stared into the fire, he studied her features. She'd separated herself from the crowd now, too, much like he had done earlier. Suddenly, it seemed she needed none of them either and he had to wonder what thoughts she contemplated as she sat there, her pert face illuminated lit by fire-glow.

His breathing labored as his gaze traveled from her face to the open neck of her borrowed western shirt, across her shoulders and down her arms to where her elbows sat perched on her knees. His heart beat a wild cadence. It only took one look for him to remember how soft she'd felt in his hands. How warm she'd felt in his arms, next to his chest. How hard he'd been with desire for her.

With her knees drawn up close, she cradled her chin in her hands and stared trancelike into the flames. If only, he thought... if only he knew what she was thinking. What she really thought about him.

If only... He might be damned tempted to take the risk.

Familiar strains of a long-ago forgotten tune broke through the crackling silence of the campfire. One of the wranglers sitting not far from Kim began strumming his guitar. Thad watched as her startled stare lifted from the flames and caught his and stayed there for several heartbeats. His heart strummed now in rhythm to the haunting tune. Thad tore his gaze away to stare from the heat of the flames into the cool depth of the night.

Desperado.

* * *

Kim jerked back to the present as the old *Eagles* melody drifted to her ears. Alert now, and conscious of everyone about her, she lifted her gaze to meet Thad's angled across the fire. Her breath caught in her throat as she wondered if he knew, if he could tell, or sense, what she had just been thinking.

Her cheeks hot from her fantasy, she knew that at the very least she could attribute their rosy glow to the fire. Only the fire was deep within her. The ring of fire sitting before each of them was nothing compared to the one raging inside her.

She'd been fantasizing about Thad. Of Thad slipping into her tent later that night. Of his hands all over her. His lips. His body. His....

Kim trembled and shook her head, glancing about once more. Thad now stared off into the night and the music drifted around them. She studied his profile as she listened to the words of the song. Are you really such a hard man, Thad Winchester? Why are you always so gruff with me?

The cowboy's melody meandered off onto the night breeze and suddenly, Thad dragged his gaze away from the distant night and planted it squarely on Kim's face. She held the connection between them for longer than was necessary. Finally, she shivered and glanced away.

A warm body scooted closer on the log, startling her, and an arm snaked around her shoulders. Confused, she struggled out of her trance and glanced sharply to her right.

"Cold?" the male voice began, almost a soft purr. Tim Rumer's fire-lit face inched closer. His breath smelled surprisingly of beer. "I'll k-keep you warm," he whispered. "Come closer."

Kim jerked and pushed away, scooting abruptly to her left. He followed.

"C'mon, Kimmy. You're sh-shivering. I'll k-keep you warm," he slurred.

She slid again and placed her palms at Tim's chest. His timing was all off. His appearance beside her was irritating. All she wanted to do was stare into the fire and think of Thad—even though she knew she could do nothing about it.

She gave Tim another small shove. "I'm not cold, Tim. I'm sitting in front of a raging fire, for God's sake. Back off." She was in no mood to fight off a drunk and felt no remorse at being blunt. He was spoiling her mood entirely.

Tim's arms crept around her again, pulling her closer. "Kim. Kim... Kim..." He nuzzled his chin against her neck. "C'mon Kimmy... Just a little snuggle."

Not wanting to make a scene, but wanting his smelly beer-body away, she shoved once more. Harder. "Go away, Tim. You're drunk. You know you're not supposed to have alcohol on this trip. Get away from me before I tell."

Tim only chuckled and came at her again. "You're a sweet little t-tattle-tale, aren't you?"

"And you're drunk," she hissed.

"No. Just feelin' good." He grasped her waist again and dipped his head. "Come f-feel good with me, Kim-Kim," he whispered, his hands groping.

"No!"

His hands were getting way too familiar, way too fast.

Kim pushed them away and stood. "I said no, dammit! Leave me alone." Her voice raised a little louder than she had wanted.

Tim stumbled to his feet. "C'mon, Kim." He lunged.

In the next instant, Thad's rock-hard body stepped between hers and Tim's. "I believe the lady said no, Rumer," he bellowed. "And I believe you're drunk."

Tim's face drew a blank, then a grin split his lips. He stumbled closer to Thad. "N-no need to git yer dander up there, cowboy. I-I only wanted a little sq-squeeze. Don't you have some dogies that need wrestlin' or somethin'?"

Kim stood helpless as Thad snatched placket of the drunk's shirt in two hands. He dragged Tim closer and peered into his face. Seconds passed as Thad's face grew tense, his hands shook, his gaze narrowed. Then, as if checking himself against his anger, he tossed the man to the ground. Tim's eyes rounded in horror.

"I want you gone come sunup, understand? Your friend can make up his own mind about leaving, but you..." Thad pointed a blunt finger at Tim, "you I don't want to see again." Thad jerked his head up, his stare piercing the night at one of his wranglers. "Ben, ride back with him. I'll settle up when I get back to the ranch."

With that, Thad turned on his heel and faced Kim. For an exceptionally long moment, he held her gaze. Without warning, he grasped her left upper arm and whirled her body toward his, briskly leading her away from the campfire.

Kim cringed at the impression he was making on her bicep. It was all she could do to keep her short legs in stride with his massive gait.

"What do you think you're doing?" she finally gasped out.

His gaze straight ahead, he answered her bluntly. "Getting you the hell out of there." He yanked her arm, pulling her closer into his side.

"Why?"

"Because I don't want you there."

Kim jerked her arm out of his grasp and stopped. "A hell of a lot you have to say about it. Are you planning to send me packing in the morning, too?"

Thad turned, parked his fists on his hips, and stared down at her. She suddenly felt minute, so small and petite next to him.

"No, goddammit. I ought to. But no."

Grasping her arm again, Thad turned and resumed his gait while Kim struggled out of his grasp every few steps.

"Wherever you're taking me, you know, you don't have to manhandle me. I can walk perfectly well of my own accord."

Ignoring her, Thad brusquely pulled her behind the kitchen tent. In one swift movement, he swung her around to face him. In that instant, Kim sensed just exactly what was on Thad's mind. It was the same thing that had been on hers moments earlier.

Without a word, both his hands cupped her face. The gruffness gone, he cradled her chin within his fingers, and tilted her face upward. In his eyes, Kim could see the desire, as well as her own, in the reflection. With a quick brush of his thumb over her lower lip, she trembled, and a shot of adrenaline burst up through her, urging her closer. And as his face lowered and his lips captured hers, her universe spun out of control.

Kim had never known such ecstasy existed. His mouth

embraced hers in an intoxicating swirl of nibbles and quick thrusts of his tongue. His hands wove their way into the nape of her hair, holding her steady for him to devour her mouth and face. Rapid breathing mingled with hurried gasps; the sharp taste of salty skin bit into her tongue as she savored his lips. Blood raced to the surface, sending every nerve ending spiraling with desire.

She clung to Thad in wanton abandon. Her arms crept upward, her hands grasped and kneaded his shoulders, pulling him closer. She pressed tight against him, feeling him hard and wanting against her belly. Thad's lips traveled from the corner of her mouth, where he left a tiny bite and trailed down the side of her neck to her collarbone. He moaned and Kim heard the soft, ragged whisper of her name on his breath, and tried not to think about how painful it sounded.

Thad lowered his hands and clasped his arms around her waist, like he never wanted to let her go. He clutched her to him as she lifted to her tiptoes while he continued the kiss. Glad for his arms around her, his kisses made her feel light as air and dizzy; she needed all the support she could get. She didn't trust her legs one bit.

Between panting breaths, pounding hearts, and a mingling of lips and tongues, Kim managed only seconds of lucidity. She was kissing Thad! And she was kissing him back more fervently than she'd ever in her life returned a kiss.

Finally, he lowered her body until her feet touched the ground again, his hands still lingered at her waist. Reluctantly, their lips parted, reaching out once, and again, for another hungry taste of each other. Her pulse racing, starbursts of light flickering behind closed eyes. She lost all sense of time and place. Of who she was, why she was here. Why her world suddenly tipped off its axis. Then she felt Thad's labored breathing warmly caress her face and knew she was alive. And wanting him. When her eyes opened, she stared into the face of the man who had just curled her toes into ribbons.

But the face she saw wasn't the Thad she'd known all week. This face was soft, vulnerable, passion-filled, and alive. Loving. And his eyes were searching her face for the same expressions. Searching for something she wasn't quite sure she could name.

Or give.

"I didn't want to do that," he murmured, still watching her face.

"I didn't want you to," she whispered back.

"I couldn't stand seeing him touch you."

"I didn't want him to touch me."

"I wanted to touch you. Had to touch you. Kiss you..."

Titillating tremors surged up within Kim. It was as though her fantasy had come true. Even if she didn't want it to. "I wanted you to touch me. Kiss me."

The dancing lights in Thad's eyes flared at her words. Urgently, he leaned closer and captured her once more in a light, but desirous meeting of the lips.

Then he drew back, abruptly.

Standing erect, Thad took a distancing step away from her, his hands dropping to his sides, the connection between them broken. For a moment, she stood watching him, her chest heaving, anticipating. He paced a couple of steps, ran his fingers through his hair.

"It can't happen again," Thad said softly. He hesitated, his gaze playing over her face, then receded into the dark. He evaporated into the night, leaving her totally alone.

She watched him leave and felt the stab in her chest, the sting in her eyes. Never had a single moment in her life affected her as this one. Never. "I know," she whispered, barely hearing the words herself. "I know."

* * *

I don't know why in the hell I didn't take her back to Durango, myself.

Thad stared into the ebony void before him. From his perch high on a ledge above the camp, he contemplated the twist of fate he'd been dealt a few hours earlier. His back rested against cold stone, keeping him alert in the chilly night, one foot propped against the rock evening out his balance. He couldn't sleep. He didn't know if he'd ever fall asleep again—without images he didn't want to acknowledge traipsing through his brain.

It was the type of night where silence crashed about you. A million stars set like sparkling diamonds into the sable sky. Nightfall was still and cool. Only an occasional cry from a night bird and the far-off whine of a coyote broke the quiet.

He loved a night like this. Calm. Restful. Usually, the feeling transferred to his own sense of inner peace. He imagined that's why men were drawn to this land, this line of work, for over a hundred years. There was nothing he could think of as relaxing as a mountain sky on a cool, starry night.

Tonight, though, the night was fickle. She failed to work her charm. He felt neither calm, nor restful.

Below, the camp lay still. Only the lantern under the dining fly was lit, granting him a guiding beacon back to camp. He threw a cautious glance behind him; occasionally a horse nickered below. Everyone else had turned in hours ago, but not him.

And he damned well knew why.

Restless energy pounded his insides. Energy that longed for escape.

Lifting a hand to his face, Thad took another long drag off the Camel he'd bummed earlier from Ben, the red ashes dancing against the black. After a moment of holding the smoke deep inside his lungs, urging the nicotine to calm his jittery nerves, he blew a thorough puff skyward. Abruptly, he glanced at the butt and flicked it to the ground, crushing the life out of the fire with the toe of his boot.

He hadn't smoked in years.

Closing his eyes, the instant image of Kim blew into his mind's view. Her damned blue eyes spoke volumes, her delicate full lips, her sweet, soft skin tasted like honey—each one more reason to stay awake. Much more and he'd be in her tent before the night was through. It was all he could do to stay away. And he wasn't too sure how her resistance was holding up either.

Dammit! He didn't think either of them could resist the pull, the chemistry—even knowing that it was the dead-wrong thing to do.

He was not about to get involved with one of his guests. Not now. He had to be patient. Wait until the end of the week. See how things progressed. Then maybe....

But resisting Kim was absolutely the hardest thing he'd ever tried to do in his life.

Hell, he'd taken women on the pack trips before. Attractive women. But never had this degree of temptation plagued him. It was Kim. He was like a moth drawn to a flame around her.

Thad washed his hands over his face as if to remove her image, then stood abruptly and glanced toward the camp. She was down there. Alone. In her tent. And as vulnerable to him as he was to her. He knew it.

He had to stay away. He would not start something until he knew for certain that there was a chance. He didn't want to risk messing up something that he had the distinct feeling might turn out to be important to him. He needed to be sure these feelings he harbored for her were not just physical desire and lust.

Somehow, the thought of loving and leaving Kim scared the

hell out of him. Particularly when come the end of the trip; she would be the one doing the leaving.

It left an ache in his chest just thinking about it.

Chapter Nine

Why can't I just sleep?

Kim turned over in her sleeping bag and stared at the far side of the dome tent. She punched her pillow then gathered it into a ball, stuffing it under her head. She was wide awake, and about as tired as she'd ever felt in her life. Besides the images of Thad kissing her dancing through her head, she didn't know what could be keeping her awake. She'd barely slept the night before.

Except that her stomach hurt. And she felt kind of dizzy. A little short of breath.

Geez, Kim, did Thad do all this to you?

"Certainly, not," she muttered. "No one man's kisses ever made me feel like this before."

Her stomach ached and she clutched at it. Beads of sweat popped out on her forehead and she tossed off the sleeping bag. "Too damn hot in here."

After several minutes of lying there, her symptoms escalating, she decided it wasn't Thad who had thrown her body a bit off kilter—she was sick.

"Damn-damn-damn," she whispered. "I don't want to be

sick. I'll die up here."

Things were jumping in her stomach. What had she eaten for dinner? That's right, the barbecued chicken. Had she poisoned the entire crew? Was it food poisoning? *Oh, God. I'll never hear the end of it.* Thad might even accuse her of trying to kill him and file a lawsuit against her!

"Great. Just what I need."

Her stomach rumbled and roiled, then lurched. Still hot and clammy, she kicked off her sweatpants bottoms, leaving on the large baggy shirt and her panties. She tried closing her eyes, willing her tummy to cooperate. *Maybe if I lie very still, all this will go away, and I'll be better in the morning.*

But it was soon apparent that wouldn't be the case. Nausea struck her in full force. Within seconds, she was up, had flung the opening to the tent out of her way, and raced behind the tent to throw up.

On her hands and knees, she wretched until the spasms finally subsided. Not much in the way of food that came up, but the bitter taste of bile nauseated her into further heaving.

Finally, with a trembling hand, she swiped at her mouth with the sleeve of her shirt and sat back on her knees.

Her body shook. She was very cold but needed a minute to gather her strength before heading back to her tent. And she wanted to make sure another wave of nausea wasn't going to hit her.

Eyes closed, she raked a hand through her damp hair and waited.

Her mind barely registered the presence of someone beside her.

"Kim," he whispered. "Here, let me help."

Weakly, she opened her eyes and watched as Thad poured some water from a canteen onto a washcloth. Then capping and laying the canteen aside, her reached for her and washed her face with the cool water as he pushed her damp hair out of the way.

She sighed and let him.

"Better?" He peered into her eyes as he gently stroked the damp cloth over her forehead and around her hairline, then down her neck.

"I think so."

"Can you walk back to the tent now?"

She nodded. For the moment, the waves of nausea had subsided.

He stood and grasped her hands, helping her to her feet. With one arm, he cradled her close as he guided her back into the tent.

She sat on the sleeping bag. He sat on his knees in front of her, taking up a huge amount of space in her tiny tent. His presence nearly sucked the very air away from her. She felt sort of lightheaded, again.

"Where are your things? I'll find you another shirt."

She pointed to the duffel bag.

"I'll turn my back. You take that one off."

Hesitantly, she did, tossing the shirt near the tent's entrance. His back was to her as he carefully went through her things and she felt a little vulnerable, sitting there almost naked, behind him. She shook off a little chill. Finally, he tossed a T-shirt her way, keeping his back to her.

She slipped it on. "Okay," she said softly.

He turned around.

"Thanks. I—I don't know what happened. I hope I didn't poison everybody."

A slow grin spread over his face. "You didn't poison anyone, Kim. I suspect you've got altitude sickness."

"Altitude sickness? You mean, I'm going to be sick the whole time?"

He shook his head. "Not likely. I'd say you'll acclimate soon enough. Have you had trouble sleeping?"

She nodded. *But I hadn't attributed it to altitude.*

"Felt a little dizzy? Short of breath?"

She shrugged. "Maybe." *But I thought you were doing that to me.*

He paused and studied her. "I think you'll probably feel better tomorrow. Drink plenty of water and eat right. Here, keep my canteen." He laid it beside the sleeping bag. "And if you can get to sleep, sleep as long as you can. Don't worry about the rest of us, we'll manage."

She gave him a slow nod. Watching him sitting across from her, gave her a sinking, yet jittery feeling in her stomach. It wasn't nausea. It was something else. The narrow grin he'd given her earlier was gone. As though he'd just realized where the two of them were—in her tent, alone.

He turned toward the tent opening and snatched up her shirt. "You try and get some sleep," he said softly.

"I will."

He reached for the tent flap.

"Thad...? Um. Why are you being so nice to me?"

She could barely see his eyes in the tent's darkness but sensed his uncertainty at her question.

"Kim... I—"

"Never mind," she interrupted. "Thanks anyway." She wasn't sure she wanted to know the answer.

He gave her one last glance, then left her alone.

* * *

When she finally emerged from her tent the next morning, the first thing she noticed was that it was extremely light outside.

The second thing that struck her was that there wasn't

much commotion going on inside the camp. In fact, the place looked darned deserted. The smell of fried bacon and strong coffee hit her as she neared the dining fly. For a moment, she thought someone had cooked breakfast. But when she saw no food waiting and glanced above her to notice that the sun was nearly overhead, indicating that noon was approaching, she deduced that they had indeed managed on their own.

Well, what a concept!

Picking up the skillet, she placed it back on the stove, stoked the dying fire and decided to add another piece of wood. Then she rummaged through the meat box to see if there happened to be any bacon left. Everyone else seemed to have disappeared, so she assumed they'd already eaten. Surely they wouldn't begrudge herself a bite to eat, would they? Even if it was almost lunch time?

Slowly, she glanced about. Where in the heck was everyone?

She found half a pound of bacon. The pan was now sizzling on the stove with fat left from someone else's breakfast, so she shrugged her shoulders and figured the heat would kill about anything and laid another two slices in the pan, watching the fat pop and crackle against the black iron skillet.

"Enough there for two?"

Kim jumped back and investigated Thad's face. Hers grew hot. Quickly, she glanced back down at the package of bacon in her hands.

"I think so."

"Good." He took the package from her and laid it on a table beside the stove. Pulling slices of bacon from each other, he carefully placed them in the fat. Surprised, Kim stepped back and watched. After a moment, he glanced up. "I'll take care of the bacon and eggs if you'll get the coffee and biscuits."

Thad turned back to his work and Kim, a bit dumbfounded,

stood and watched. After a second, he glanced up in question and Kim nodded and headed for the coffeepot.

She made short work of the caffeine, setting the percolator on a free burner on the stove. Two days ago, she wouldn't have guessed Thad even knew what a skillet looked like.

After rummaging around in the cold box of food again, Kim came up with a can of refrigerator biscuits. She popped the cardboard container and placed each biscuit in the bottom of a round pan, all the while stealing wondering glances at Thad as he turned the bacon and cracked eggs.

She picked up the pan of biscuits.

"If you'll scoot over, I'll slide these in the oven."

He looked at her then, stopping any motion he was making with his hands, and slowly slid to his right. His gaze never left her eyes.

Keeping the connection, Kim stepped beside him. She could feel his hard body just centimeters from her back. Static electricity jumped between them. For a moment, he didn't move. She didn't either. With jerky movements and shaking hands, Kim opened the oven door, slid the biscuits inside, quickly closed it again, and then awkwardly stepped back. Rubbing her hands along her thighs, she glanced his way, then averted her gaze and stepped away. "Those shouldn't take long, the oven's pretty hot," she threw over her shoulder.

Thad who hadn't moved from his spot. The air between them seemed crackled. "Bacon's done," he said. "Eggs will be ready in a minute." Then he turned back to his task, whisked the eggs, and after draining all but a bit of fat from the pan, dumped the egg mixture into the skillet with a sizzle.

Kim swallowed hard and sat at the camp table, her back to the table's edge, facing Thad. This was awkward. Hours before, he had run his fingers through her hair and raked his lips across hers, fiercely as well as gently, sending her into a spiral of emotion. Then he'd walked away, disappeared into the night, and told her it could never happen again.

And then deep into the night, he'd come to her. He'd cooled her feverish face and had taken care of her when she needed help. So many confusing thoughts and conflicting emotions bounced around inside her.

All night she'd dreamed of lying in his arms.

All night long she'd told herself it was impossible. Nothing good could ever come of a brief fling in this mountain paradise. In a few days, she was going home.

To her potential house on the east side and her secure, stable future.

To her future husband, whom she'd just not met yet.

To her future children, whom she'd not yet conceived.

To her Junior League meetings

To her mom and dad.

Her job.

Suddenly, all that seemed so distant, so far removed from what she was experiencing now. So everyday typical that what was happening to her now seemed exciting, atypical. She hadn't realized how mundane her life back in Kentucky had become.

But now, here he was, this gorgeous cowboy, doing the thing that she was supposed to be doing. Cooking breakfast. Looking sexy as hell. And melting her insides like a Popsicle on a hot August afternoon.

Quickly, she glanced around her again.

"Where is everyone?"

Thad lifted the scrambled eggs out of the pan and scooped generous portions onto two plates. He set the skillet aside, and without a glance in her direction, opened the oven door. "Biscuits are done." He ignored her question.

Kim rose and went to the stove. With a potholder, she removed the biscuits from the oven and set them on the stove top. With a fork, she placed two biscuits on each plate. As her hand reached to lift the plates, so did Thad's. Fingers touched. Hips bumped. The tension between them sizzled like cracklings in hot fat.

Kim gulped and jerked back her hands. Thad lifted the plates from the table.

"I'll get these. You get the coffee."

Kim did just that. After pouring two mugs full of the steaming black liquid, she followed Thad to the table and sat across from him, placing one cup by his plate. Thad dug in.

Suddenly, Kim was no longer hungry. She stared at the plate of eggs and bacon and biscuits. Her stomach did flip-flops.

"What's the matter? Still afraid of a few fat grams?"

Kim looked into his face. "Oh, no." She shook her head violently.

"Need something else, then? Ketchup for your eggs? Jam for your biscuits?"

Kim shook her head again. "No, this looks great."

"Cream for your coffee?" A broad smile spread across Thad's face and Kim felt her insides mesh.

"No." She rubbed a hand across her stomach.

Thad stopped chewing and paused for a moment, staring at her. "Are you still sick?"

She shook her head.

Because you make me nervous, Thaddeus Winchester. *Because when I look at you I get butterflies in my belly and tingles all up and down my spine.* No, Kim told herself. She wasn't going to make this worse than it was already.

Grasping her fork, she forced a smile. "I was just...just reflecting on how peaceful the morning is before I settle down to eat breakfast." She glanced outside the dining fly, realizing how hokey that sounded. She turned back to Thad, puzzled. "I have to ask you a question."

Thad took a bite of biscuit and chewed slowly. "Yes...?"

"Why the abrupt change of attitude? You realize you're making me crazy here? One minute you're gruff as an old bear, the next you're fixing me breakfast. I don't understand."

Thad studied her. "Crazy? Hmm, I can identify. Let's just say... Well, I've come to a decision."

"And what decision is that?"

"That... That this old bear needed to extend a paw."

"I don't understand."

He nodded, pushed his plate back, and crossed his arms in front of him on the table. "Yeah. Me, either."

She studied him a moment longer, then glanced away. The camp was so damn still. Everything had changed. Thad. Everything. Eerie. She turned back.

"Where is everyone?"

Thad's gaze met hers like a rock to the gut. "Everyone? Oh, they're gone. Mostly."

* * *

He had to be honest with her.

If he hadn't been anything else, at least she could go away from here saying he'd been that—honest. If she had half a brain, which he suspected she did, she had to know how he felt about her after last night.

He had to hold on a few more days. He had to keep his feelings for her under wraps until then. But there was no reason to be unkind to her.

Thad watched the panic flare in Kim's widened eyes.

"Gone? Where?" Her voice cracked.

He tried to respond in as direct a manner as he could manage. "Most, anyway. Mack and Jillie went out on a little excursion this morning."

113

"I'll just bet they did," Kim muttered.

"They took the couple from Rhode Island with them."

"I see."

Thad knew she was trying to keep her emotions in check.

"And the others?"

"Ben rode back with the lawyers earlier. Your friend Tim decided he'd played city slicker long enough. I told Bed to stay at the ranch. Luke is still around here somewhere, tending to the animals, and overseeing the other wranglers. I figure Mack and I can handle you and Jillie quite fine by ourselves."

"So we're finishing the trip?"

"Yes. We are."

Again, a hint of alarm played around Kim's eyes. Thad tried to read her expression, but it was hard. Panic coursed up inside himself. Just why in tarnation had he used that choice of words?

Damn. The next several days were going to be long. It was all he could do to tear his gaze away from Kim's beautiful face. And he was half afraid that if he ever got her in his arms again, nothing would stop him from taking his fill of her, either.

That's why it couldn't happen. Not yet. She fueled a different kind of hunger deep within him each time those damnable blue eyes met his.

"So, where are Jillie and Mack off to?" Her question broke his thoughts.

"Looking for bones."

"Bones? *Bones?*" Her brow arched.

"Some members of a pack trip we lost last year." Thad knew he shouldn't have said the words the second they were out of his mouth.

"What?"

Kim's high-pitched voice pierced the quiet, and Thad jerked up his head in amusement. She had the most frightened look about her, soft and innocent at the same time. Her short blond haircut furled around her head in a rather unkempt fashion, which made her appear even more impish. Her eyes were round as biscuits. He wanted to laugh out loud but was afraid she'd deck him from across the table. His heart felt full and heavy. She was so damned beautiful, so gullible.

"Just kidding. They're looking for bones from an early Fremont expedition."

* * *

There was a twinkle in Thad's eye that Kim had never seen before. If she hadn't been so alarmed a moment earlier, she might have thought his little joke funny. But the simple fact remained that his joking was cause for warning. She would never have dreamed Thad could possess a sense of humor. And it was not only charming, but shocking, because if this little hint of humor could crack some of that gruff exterior, then, well....

Then she was in a lot of trouble. She didn't want him teasing her. Teasing led to flirting. And flirting led to other things. And those other things were going to get her into trouble if she let him get too close.

Be civil to the man, Kim. Keep your distance. And don't fall into the flirting game. Then you'll be safe.

"Oh," she replied in a matter-of-fact voice. "John Fremont, I presume. Wasn't that during the...let's see, about the mid-1840s?"

A few days earlier, Kim would have been out to prove she was about a whole lot more than manicured nails and expensive haircuts. Even though those things were important to her. She'd wanted to prove that she could pull her weight, just like the rest of the crew. But now, well, everything was getting all mixed up. One minute she didn't want him to know diddly squat about her, the other she was trying to impress him with her cooking and her brain; and then the next she's telling herself to stop flirting so it won't bring on any more of his wonderful kisses. Oh, God....

What is happening here?

Thad's face grew serious and as he spoke about the expedition. "About 1840, I think. A little earlier than his expeditions through the upper Rockies and Oregon. You know that's how Starvation Gulch got its name, don't you? I can't remember all the particulars. Talk to Mack if you're interested, but I think quite a bit of his party was lost during that expedition. Starved to death, I imagine. Mack's been itching to take some of the guests out on a side trip to play amateur archeologist. I guess that's what he and Jillie are doing today."

"Yeah, I bet," Kim mumbled and glanced past Thad's head. If she knew Jillie, searching for old bones was the last thing on her mind. Jumping Mack's bones was more like it.

"Why do you say that?"

She shook her head, her cheeks heating up. "Uh, never mind." She shifted on the bench, picked up a biscuit and took a bite. "So," she said a moment later, trying to act very nonchalant. "What are your plans for the afternoon?"

An awkward silence fell between them. Both their gazes met. Kim picked up the biscuit again and took another bite. The consistency of the bread was crumbly, making it difficult to chew. Or was it that her mouth and lips had suddenly gone dry? Finally, she swallowed, coaxing the bread down with a sip of hot coffee. At least it was wet.

"We have the afternoon to ourselves, I guess."

Kim looked to her plate, suddenly ravenous, and shoveled a bite of cold scrambled eggs into her mouth. What was he suggesting?

"Anything you would like to do?"

She knew if she looked up at him, he would know exactly what she would like to do. But they would not do *that*.

She swallowed the eggs and lifted her face. "You're sure we're alone?"

With his gaze locked on hers, he dropped his head in slow nod. Maybe a little alarm crossed his eyes. For a split-second, she lost sight of those fathomless orbs when his cowboy hat dipped lower. Then suddenly, there they were again.

Piercing. Questioning. Playful.

What was he doing? Playing her for a fool? Was he ready for her to spring on him only so he could knock her down again like he did last night? Well, she wasn't going to fall for that old hat trick, was she?

Not a muscle in Thad's jaw jerked. His lips were taut and thin and straight as straw. He looked sexy as hell.

Oh, hell, I'm a goner.

She had no earthly idea what he intended, but she knew exactly what he wanted. And what he didn't want. And that she didn't want it either. Did she?

God help them.

Kim raked a hand through her unruly, dirty hair. "I... What I'd really like, Thad. I think I'd... I'd like to take a bath."

Thad straightened in his seat and eyed. "A bath."

"Yes."

If he said one word about being a prissy little socialite, she'd blast him, Kim decided right then and there. It had been days since she'd felt clean and if she didn't immerse her entire body into water soon, she figured she'd rot about any second. And the more she thought about, the more she decided she wouldn't be denied.

Besides, a cold dip in the stream might keep her mind off warm sleeping bags and muscled arms wrapped around her. Involuntarily, she shivered.

But as her gaze met his, she saw nothing in his eyes that was the least bit condescending. What she saw was raw, reined-in hunger.

Oh. God.

Standing, Thad stepped back from the table, as though to end any conversation taking turns down paths he'd rather not venture and peered down at her. Glancing at his plate, Kim realized he'd finished his meal long ago. She'd barely touched her own.

"Okay," he said, moving away from her. "I've got some things to do around the camp, so you go for it. I'll move the stock. Pack up some of the gear we won't be using now. In fact, I'll clean up the kitchen tent."

"I can do that. You cooked," Kim amended, rising.

Thad shook his head and put out his hands. Kim wondered if it was an attempt to put up a physical barrier between them. "No. You've been cooking and cleaning all week. I'll do it. Take your bath. It's probably a rather good time for you to do that. You remember the rules?"

Kim threw a blank look his direction before recalling his pre-trip instructions about not altering the environment in any way. The proper way to latrine. To clean the dishes. Take care of the garbage. To bathe. "Yes. I remember." She had no desire to spoil the pristine beauty of the land surrounding her.

"Good. There's an extra basin in the supply box over there. You know where the stream is. Take as long as you wish. No one will bother you."

There was an awkward, tentative crackle in the air about them as Kim met his eyes, nodded, and retreated from under the dining fly. *No one will bother you.* His words rang loud and true in her ear.

The thing was, she wasn't entirely sure she wanted to be left alone.

Chapter Ten

T had worked around the kitchen tent for a while, avoiding looking in the direction of Kim's tent. He didn't want to imagine her there, preparing for her bath. And when he heard her walk past, heading toward the stream, he purposely pointed his gaze toward the basin full of suds and dirty dishes so he could keep his mind on his task. But when he'd figured she'd just about reached the area where a stand of trees bordering the stream would cut off his view of her, he tipped his head up to stare across the horizon after her.

He caught just a glimpse of her golden-blonde head and her back as she disappeared through the trees, a towel thrown over her shoulder.

Why had he acted the way he had earlier? What had possessed him to literally tease and flirt, when the night before he'd practically told her he wanted nothing to do with her? Did he want a reaction out of her? Did he want her to banter back and forth with him? Did he want her to come to him, to make love with him? Was that what he was intimating when he'd made the comment about them being alone?

Probably, you loco SOB. You want time alone with her; you want to get to know her better. And not just her body.

Intrigued as he'd been by her pert beauty, he was also fascinated with the woman herself. And the feelings he had for her were going a lot deeper than he really wanted.

The next thirty minutes or so he tried to erase those thoughts from his brain and busied himself with feeding and moving the picketed horses, packing up a few unnecessary items, and burning some of their refuse. He tried like hell to obliterate any and all images of what might happen on the other side of that stand of pines out of his mind.

Impossible.

Straightening his body from where he'd just compiled two boxes of food into one, Thad let his gaze rest on the area where he knew Kim was bathing. His eyes closed and inhaled deeply, imaging the scent of floral-essence shampoo penetrating his nostrils, and the feel of water-softened skin under his palms.

He imagined Kim standing naked on the stream bank, her body and hair slick with water and soap as she poured a basinfull over her head, letting the crystal-clear water sluice over her skin. Glistening in the sunlight, her hands raised to her face, where she pushed tiny droplets out of her eyes with her fingers, then threaded them straight back over her head, squeezing the excess water from her hair. Her breasts, peaked and raised toward the sun seemed to jut out into the Rocky Mountain atmosphere like they belonged there, a part of the natural surroundings. In his mind, Thad reached out. Touched her.

A tremor ran through his body.

Shaking his head, the image disappeared. For a second. At the realization he was fantasizing, he also grasped the fact that there was a growing hardness developing just south of his belt. Desire for Kim coursed through him. Because of his thoughts and dreams of her the past few days, these feelings—this passion, obsession, he felt toward her—could no longer be ignored. He was going to have to do something about her. One way or another.

* * *

"This is heaven."

Immediately upon shedding her clothing, Kim waded in and sank to her neck in the water, letting the cool mountain stream slide over her body. With her arms draped over two nearby boulders, she leaned into the rocks and settled herself quite comfortably between them, letting her head fall back and her eyes close.

The water was cool, almost cold at times, but she didn't care. The longer she stayed in, she got used to it and it felt wonderful. The grime, dust, and smoke seemed to ooze out of her pores. It was the most relaxing thing she'd experienced during the entire trip. Blue sky above. Small wispy clouds. Only the sound of the rushing water at ear-level.

The days of hell she'd endured prior to this moment were almost worth getting to experience this small piece of heaven now. She'd almost, almost, do it again.

Hell? Was that what this was?

Eyes closed, she reminisced the events of the past three days. The trail ride was a disaster. The breakfast at the Flying W was even worse. The first day of riding she'd been so damned saddle sore she thought it would be better to die. And then, to fall into her sleeping bag and into Thad Winchester's arms was almost more than she could stand.

Shaking herself, she opened her eyes to stare into the sky above her. Even in the cold water, her body was becoming aroused at the thought of her and Thad sharing the same sleeping bag.

And his kisses. Oh, she'd felt lost when he'd kissed her. Her body had responded with unabashed passion. She'd wanted him to stay. Wanted him to come to her later that night.

And didn't want him at the same time.

There could be no future between her and a Colorado cowboy. There was nothing to happen between the two of them and she really wasn't the kind for a vacation romance. She couldn't wait to get back to Kentucky. To the security of her own little world. Where she was safe.

Safe? From a man whom she obviously had feelings for and who apparently had feelings for her?

So why was she lying here, fantasizing about how good his arms felt around her and what his kisses did to her insides, thinking about escaping to her safe little life back in Kentucky?

She didn't know.

It was hell. A hell of her own making.

But the thought kept nagging. What *would* be the problem if she and Thad entered into some kind of relationship? The problem, she deduced, was that their two worlds just would not mesh. Rather, they would collide, and it would be an ugly collision.

She'd worked hard to earn her counseling degree and it was the one thing she felt proud of, the one thing that excited her about getting up in the morning. Her students were important to her, they depended on her, and she on them, sometimes probably too much, to make her life seem worthwhile.

What would be here for her in this mountain wilderness? Ranch life? Heck, she could barely ride old Sunshine, what kind of a ranch wife would she be?

She startled herself at that thought. Wife? Why would she even think that? There was nothing between her and Thad but some overactive hormonal activity. In fact, maybe if they just went on and got it out of their systems, then all the agonizing would be over with and they could enjoy the rest of the trip. Perhaps....

No, even if that thought brought enticing images to her mind, she couldn't let that happen. Could she?

After a half an hour or so, Kim rose from the stream, not really wanting to lather up and rinse on the bank as Thad had instructed before they'd left the Flying W. She recalled his instructions to the letter. "Soap is soap, no matter how biodegradable," he'd told them. "We don't want to spoil the natural environment, so we take pains not to. By soaping and rinsing on the bank, we can avoid directly putting the detergents into the clean mountain water, letting the soil naturally filter any pollutants."

As much concerned about the environment as the next person, she'd always taken care to buy products which would not hurt the environment, such as biodegradable soaps and detergents. She recycled her newspapers and soda cans and took care to conserve water. And glancing around her, she hated to think of anyone spoiling this beauty with trash and chemicals.

But oh, wouldn't it feel so damn good to bathe in this cool, meandering stream?

Begrudgingly, she rose from the water and approached the bank. After retrieving the wash basin, she dipped it into the stream and filled it with water, then carried it up the bank. There she quickly soaped her body then splashed and poured water from the basin over her to rinse. Now for her hair, she thought, which felt incredibly gritty and oily.

Picking up her shampoo, she stared at the bottle and longed to plunge her head and body into the stream and wash and rinse until the last bit of grime was lifted from her scalp and washed away. How was she going to get her hair clean, lathering and rinsing up here on the bank?

She bit her lip and stared toward the camp.

No. She wouldn't.

She peered down at the shampoo bottle. Nature's Essence. Rose petal scent. Made from natural herbs and plants. Turning the bottle over, her gaze trailed down to the ingredients list at the bottom. She grinned. Certainly, a shampoo composed of all-natural plant materials and dyes could do no damage to the environment, could it?

Absolutely not.

Convinced now, she decided she'd use only a minute amount. Just enough to cleanse her hair and give it some bounce again. And to smell that rose petal scent, well, it might give her just the tiny bit of luxury she needed to get through the rest of the trip.

She glanced once more at the camp. She couldn't see on the other side of the pines, but she knew Thad was back there. He'd promised she'd not be bothered. There was no reason she shouldn't enjoy a bit of pampering now, was there?

He would never know.

Quickly, she turned back toward the stream, shampoo bottle in hand.

Wading into deeper water than before, she sat the bottle on a rock. Ducking beneath the surface to wet her hair again, she came up and swiped the excess water out of her eyes before she reached for the shampoo and squeezed a dime-sized mound into her palm.

The water moved past at her hip level. She raised her hands and gently massaged the shampoo into her hair.

Luxuriating in the feel of the silky soft bubbles in her hands, rubbing them fully into her scalp, she closed her eyes and sighed as the lather made trails down her shoulders and breasts.

"Ahh..." she whispered, "I did not know how wonderful it would feel to finally be clean all over."

The rose scent wafted over her, making her feel both

pampered and sexy. She breathed deeply, her fingers delicately massaging her scalp. After a moment, she lowered herself closer to the water, rinsing the bubbles from her shoulders, and running her hands down her body to splash away any excess lather. After that, she fully ducked beneath water's surface again to rid her hair of the shampoo.

When she rose from the water, she spied the bottle on the rock. Kim spontaneously stood and reached for it, and without thinking, popped the lid and drizzled the creamy pink lotion over her arms and breasts and belly.

Suddenly, she felt deliciously wicked and seductive.

Her movements were slow and methodical. One hand rose to her neck as she lifted her head toward the sky, closed her eyes, and breathed deeply of the crisp mountain air. Her fingers carefully caressed her skin as they trailed closer to her breasts. Upon contact with the slippery shampoo, the pads of her fingers glided over the mound of first one breast, then another, her other hand joining in the gentle caress. The lather from the shampoo bubbled through her fingers as she felt her breasts grow taut, her nipples already pebble hard and alert from the cool water.

As she cupped both breasts, she threw her head back further as the image of Thad burst into her mind. He was standing behind her. She was breathing heavily. And it was his large, rough hands caressing her breasts, pinching her nipples, and causing the desire to race up within her, not hers. A small moan escaped her lips as when in her fantasy, his hands lowered to her belly and massaged the pink shampoo into her skin. He pulled her tight against his hard, unclothed male body, causing tremors to erupt inside her as his fingers snaked lower.

"Oh, Thad..." she rasped, going fully with the fantasy.

She slid lower into the water, her knees buckling, imagining

Thad lowering her into his sleeping bag. She could feel his lips on the back of her neck.

Hot. Breathy. Biting.

"Oh, Thad," she breathed again.

"Oh, Thad, what?" came the stern voice from not far away.

* * *

It was his fantasy come to life.

At first, he'd risked only a glimpse through the pines. But the second he caught sight of her, he couldn't pull away. No matter how much he wanted to, or how hard he tried. Which anymore, really wasn't that much.

He was held spellbound by her beauty. Mesmerized by her delicate features against the harsh, craggy mountains. Entranced by the way her fingers and hands slid over her silky skin. Bewitched by her expression, eyes closed, lips mumbling soft, incoherent words to the sun.

As he'd stepped through the trees, he knew she could see him, should she decide to open her eyes. He knew he was taking steps which he may not be able to retract. He knew that one way or another, if she did open her eyes and see him standing there, watching her, that things between them would never be the same.

He knew there would be no turning back.

His gaze was drawn to the lather sliding down her body, clinging in luxurious bubbles to her satiny smooth skin. Her fingers caressed and teased her breasts, then slid lower to her belly. Her chin raised to the sky and he watched as her chest lifted in tiny pants and her lips opened slightly, sucking in shallow sips of air.

And in his mind he mimicked every movement she made with his own fingers, his own hands. They burned with want of touching her, teasing her. His lips ached to taste, his teeth to nibble.

Hellfire and damnation.

What was he doing? Deep inside, every primal urge known to man churned and thrashed. His palms ached to hold her flesh. His fingers craved to rake through her hair, to sluice the last bit of lather from her body. Every corpuscle he possessed had surged to one, throbbing area of his body and his brain had lost all ability to think coherently.

Thad jerked his gaze away from her body, as painful as it was, and paced several feet to the left. He had to leave. He couldn't stay one second longer. His out-of-control libido was something he had to deal with.

His gaze rested again on Kim.

Lather. Puddles of soap. Floating down the stream.

She was mumbling. Saying his name?

He stepped forward, listening, just to be sure. He spied the shampoo bottle on the rock. Damn.

He needed an excuse. He needed…something. His desire for her was racing out of control.

Maybe he could channel that desire into something else.

Anger? What else was new?

And there was only one thing he could be angry with her about, at this very moment. She had purposely undermined his orders.

She slid lower into the stream. "Oh, Thad…" she breathed. He didn't like the passion in her voice. It made him that much more aroused.

"Oh, Thad, what?"

Her eyes snapped open. A look of utter horror flashed over her face. And within the matter of about half a second, she plunged beneath the water. The lather lifted from her body and rushed down the stream.

He waited a second or two longer, and finally, she surfaced. Her head timidly stuck up out of the water.

"What the hell do you think you're doing? Get out of there," he barked.

"I'm taking a bath. Go away," she shouted from the stream. "You promised!"

"You're finished. Did you forget how I told you to bathe? There was to be no soap in the stream."

"I didn't forget, you moron. It's all natural. Completely biodegradable. Look." Kim reached to the rock, grasped the shampoo bottle, and hurled it.

It hit Thad just above his right knee.

"Sorry."

Thad glared at the soapy ring on his thigh, then lifted his stern gaze her way. "You've had long enough. Now, get out. You've already disobeyed my orders. I want to make sure you don't do it again."

That word obey just didn't sit well. Kim took a moment to assess the situation. Her fondling fantasy notwithstanding, she had nothing to be embarrassed about. She'd done nothing wrong. He had no reason to speak to her in such a manner.

"I'm not finished." She turned her head and swam a little further out.

"You are finished."

"I don't think so."

"I do think so."

"I'll leave when you leave."

"You'll leave when I tell you."

She'd had just about enough of his male macho, caveman antics. "Go to hell," she tossed back.

Thad threw up his hands. "I'm already in hell!"

She giggled under her breath. Thad was obviously as frustrated by the entire situation as she. But the devil in her took over. She could hardly resist teasing him. Tempting him. Forcing his hand on this issue.

And besides, she might just enjoy teasing him. Baiting him. Tempting him.

She wanted him to come in after her.

"It's only hell if you say so, Thad." She stood. The water rushed by at her waist, making a trailing vee in the water. She faced him fully. And for once, knew exactly what she was doing. "If you want me out of the water, then come in and get me."

Silently, she prayed. If he walked away from her this time, it would be all over. She'd walk back to the damn ranch herself, if she had to, but she'd not stay one moment longer in his presence. Why she was putting herself through this humiliation, she didn't know. She was working on instinct, here, pure and simple. She had no earthly idea where it would lead.

Nor did she care.

His eyes met hers and bore deep. Even though several yards of water and earth separated them, a beacon connected them. She was breathing hard. She knew he was too. Then his chest heaved once more, and Kim was sure he'd decided.

He took his hat off and tossed it to the ground.

Oh God. Lust coursed up within her.

He stepped forward.

Two, then three steps more and he was in the water. Slowly, he made his way toward her, his eyes never leaving hers. She watched as he drew nearer, each step he took rivaling the slow drum of her heart. Pounding. Stepping. Coming.

Breathe, Kim. Breathe.

He was inches away and her gaze traveled over him. His face searched hers. Both their breathing was heavily laced with anticipation. Each knew that with the first touch, there would be no turning back. Kim knew that. She knew he knew it, too.

And then he touched her.

Gently, at first, his fingertips grazed her cheek. Kim closed her eyes and relished in the feel of his warm fingers on her cool skin. Then he cupped her cheek and her eyes flashed open.

Here she was, naked to the world, and Thad up to his thighs in wet clothing. But between them, there seemed to be nothing more. Nothing between them but those physical barriers of his clothing. No pretense. Nothing else seemed to exist.

He reached to the back of her head and pulled her closer. His free arm circled her back and hauled her up against him. Roughly, his lips fell upon hers like a scavenger upon his prey. Warm, sensual, soft—she tasted, pressing into him. Smooth and sexy, his cheeks held a hint of morning stubble. Exciting her. Stimulating her. Never again would a smooth, bare face hold the enticement it once had. Not after kissing Thad.

A thrill rushed up and she wrapped her arms around him. His palms raced over her. Molding. Teasing. His lips devoured her lips, her face, her neck. Her soul. The breath whooshed from her; she trailed wet kisses over his face, behind his ear. Panting. Huffing. Sucking in sweet breaths laced with his essence.

Wild. Wonderful. Sensual. Gritty. Male.

Lord, she was a goner.

In one smooth movement, he lifted her into his arms and out of the water. His mouth never left hers as he carried her toward solid earth. He set her down on a crumpled towel and covered her body with his.

Urgent. Needy. Wanting.

He raked hot kisses from her chin to her chest.

"Ah...Kimmy," he whispered, coarse and low. "God, what you're doing to me."

"Don't...stop," she urged.

Moaning, his hand palmed a breast and his mouth lowered to take her nipple into his mouth. Arching against him, Kim thrust her breasts skyward, urging him to take her, as fully as possible, relishing in the feel of his mouth taking in her flesh. He suckled, gently, hungrily. Fully.

She wanted more.

"Thad," she whispered. "Look at me."

He lifted his head and gazed into her face. She traced his lips with her thumb, explored his passion-filled face, then dipped her finger inside his mouth and circled his tongue. Lunging for her lips, Thad took her mouth again, tongues mingled in hot delight as Kim slid her hands between their chests so she could gain access to the buttons of his shirt.

Rough, ripping, she jerked them free, one by one, then tugged and pulled at his damp shirt until it was gone. She threw her head back as he slid over her, her hands molding the contours of his rugged, muscled chest. Black, shiny hairs laced with silver clung to her fingers as she caressed and kneaded his firm flesh. Pulling up, she flicked her tongue over one nipple, felt it jump pebble hard, and then laved with the flat part over his entire chest, like a wild animal licking her mate.

Thad shuddered and fell upon her. His heavy body weighted against her as he moved lower and Kim struggled, reaching lower, to find the buckle to his belt.

She wanted more. All of him.

All the dandies in the world couldn't give her this.

His mouth made a hot, moist path from one breast to another. Then lower, to her belly. Her navel. Torturing sweet caresses he made with his tongue. Lower, to the triangular patch at the junction of her thighs....

"Kim! Thad! Where in the hell are you guys?"

Jillie's shout echoed through her like a freight train screeching to a reckless halt. Her eyes flashed open, suddenly aware of her vulnerability. Thad scrambled backward. For a millisecond, their gazes caught, then Thad grabbed his shirt and hastily put it on. Kim savored the lingering glance. She had an idea what was coming next.

"Kim? Thad?"

"Sorry," he muttered. "This never should have happened. I guess... I guess we... I just got carried away." He gave her one last lingering look of apology, then turned and loped off in the opposite direction.

Yeah. Me too.

Kim picked up her own clothing and got dressed.

* * *

Thad jerked the cinch on his horse and the animal side-stepped a little. Immediately, he felt guilty and whispered calming words into the gelding's ear. No reason to take out his frustrations on the animal. After mounting the buckskin, he twisted in the saddle upon hearing Mack's voice.

"Where're you off to, Winchester?"

Thad leveled his gaze at Mack. "What the hell business is it of yours, Montgomery? Seems you've got enough to keep your mind and hands occupied."

Mack stepped closer to the horse but stayed silent.

"In fact," Thad added, "it seems to me there's a little matter about camp rules we need to discuss."

Mack glanced away. "I don't know what you're talking about."

"The hell you don't. You're too old to play stud pup. Either reign in your so obvious infatuation with that girl or we're calling off the trip."

Mack met his gaze. "You'd like to do that, wouldn't you? It

would give you an excuse to end the torture you're dealing Kim and yourself." He stepped closer. Thad ignored the obvious dig. "Look. I've been discreet with Jillie up until this morning. Now that the wranglers and the other guests are gone, it's just the four of us. Why make an issue out of it?"

"Because it's good business sense not to play hanky-panky with the guests, Mack. And you know it."

Mack crossed his arms over his chest and eyed Thad. "What's really eating you, Thad?"

Thad snorted and cast his gaze toward the mountain stream where moments earlier he'd made a fool of himself. Again. What was eating him? That he'd damned near broken his one hard-and-fast rule might have something to do with it. Or was it something else.

"Nothing."

"Oh, right. I've forgotten. You're always this pleasant."

Thad returned his gaze. "Stay out of it. It's none of your business."

"That's right."

"I don't need any advice from you."

"Right again," Mack amended.

"I can handle my own damned problems."

"And quite well, I might add."

Thad threw Mack a venomous look. "I'm going for a ride. Be back before dark. You and... And our guests start packing up everything you can. We're heading to Elk Park, tomorrow."

"Tomorrow?"

"That's what I said. Straight through."

Mack grasped Thad's stare. "If that's what you want."

"It is." Thad pressed his thighs into the horse. The sooner they got off this mountain, the sooner he'd get Kim alone. Preferably in his bed.

"Thad. It won't hurt to admit that you're intrigued a little bit by her. That you might even like her."

Like her? He a hell of a lot more than liked her. He didn't need some lovesick cowboy pointing that out. In fact, he could very easily admit that he was attracted to Kim more than he'd ever been attracted to any woman. Hell, if he let himself, he might even love her. And even making love with her really wasn't the real problem. What worried him, was what came later, when Miss Kim Martin decided it was time to go home.

Chapter Eleven

"You enjoy your afternoon?" Jillie whispered to Kim as she stirred a pot of stew. Mack was tending the stock. Kim had no earthly idea where Thad had gone. All she knew was that his horse was gone as well. Good. She wasn't in the mood to spar with them both. Jillie was about to drive her crazy.

Kim flashed her a warning look and stepped away.

Jillie hedged closer.

"You can talk to me, Kim." She sidled next to her while Kim buttered thick slices of bread for toast. "Fill me in on the details? Mack said Thad was, irritated, to say the least. I can tell when something's up. Er, I mean...we didn't interrupt anything, did we?" She batted her eyes innocently.

Again, Kim shot her a narrow-eyed glance. She wasn't in the mood to talk about it. Or for Jillie's sexual innuendoes. And talk about it she would not. After all, she'd already decided to pretend that nothing had happened. And if she didn't verbalize any of it, well, then, it never really did happen.

Except that her brain wasn't so easily tricked. Or her body.

Her brain knew what had happened. Along with her lips, her breasts, her....

"So, Jillie...did you snag any big bones this afternoon?" Kim turned the tables with a saccharin smile.

Jillie held her gaze for just a moment. "One," she returned calmly, smiling. "Mack said it was unusually large. Inhuman probably. Very unusual. Maybe even prehistoric in nature." Jillie struck a puzzled pose. "Some sort of evolved Homo erectus thing. Perhaps Bigfoot, even. You know he's into all that archaeology stuff."

"Yeah, I'll bet it was erectus," Kim muttered and turned to slide the toast into the hot oven, trying her best to ignore Jillie.

"Mack's such a romantic, though. Did you see the wildflowers he picked for me this afternoon?"

How could I miss them, Jillie, you waved them in my face all afternoon.

"I'll bet Thad's just like him. Did you know he and Mack have been friends since they were kids? You should get them talking some time about all their shenanigans growing up. It's a hoot just to listen to Mack. Thad really is an okay guy, Kim."

For once, Kim wished Jillie would just shut up. She didn't need her going on about how wonderful a guy Thad was. She'd suspected that all along. She guessed she just hit on a nerve with him that threw them both out of whack instantly. But knowing that Thad was such a wonderful guy only added to her problems. It was hard to leave wonderful guys behind.

Jillie droned on, and Kim barely comprehended a word. This camping thing was getting old. Listening to what a wonderful guy Mack is, was also getting old. And Jillie's constant putting of Thad on a pedestal was just about older than anything.

She didn't want to hear it anymore.

Kim ladled the stew into a big serving bowl. "Yeah, well,

Thad's just one peachy guy. Mack, too." Kim threw Jillie a silencing look. "And in case you haven't noticed, I really don't want to talk about it anymore. Okay?"

Jillie halted, stopping her jaw in mid-motion. "Well, I didn't realize I'd hit a nerve."

In frustration, Kim set the stew on the camp table, just a mite too hard, and planted her fists on her hips. "Jillie, you've hit just about every nerve I possess in the past five minutes. No, make that the past five days." She placed her hand under her chin. "And I've had it about up to here with cowboys and horses and sleeping bags and digging holes for latrines. I want out of this damned camp site so bad I could just about sprout wings and fly. If I had but one wish it would be to get back to Kentucky as soon as possible and never step one foot on Colorado soil again. I will never forgive you for tricking me into this, do you understand? I may just never forgive you!"

Blessed silence fell between them. Thank God. She finally shut up, Kim thought. But then she took in her friend's startled gaze and regretted her every word.

Kim huffed out a long breath. "Jillie, look. I'm sorry. It's just that—"

She watched Jillie's gaze skitter off to her right.

"You'll have your wish soon enough," came the voice from behind.

Kim whirled and came face to face with Thad. His hooded eyes glinted like black diamonds.

"What?"

"We're leaving in the morning. I'd say you'll be back home by noon tomorrow. Now, where's dinner?"

Turning, Thad headed for the table and sat. Mack followed like an obedient puppy. And Jillie reached for the toast in the oven.

Dumbfounded, Kim stood and watched the entire scenario.

Sheesh! The almighty Winchester had spoken, and the peons jumped.

Damn them. Damn them all.

She turned on her heel and left.

* * *

Needing a few minutes to collect her thoughts, Kim marched straight up into a small grove of trees and plopped right down at the base of a tall pine. She had a great view of the dining fly. Damn them. Sitting there eating like absolutely nothing has happened.

What *had* happened?

She dropped her head into her hands. Well, for one, she nearly made love with Thad. Right out in the open. On the ground. Like a... Like a savage, or something. That's what happened.

And then there was the bit about him running away again. What is it with that man? What is it with her? Why is he always leaving and why did she not want him to?

Why am I so upset when he does?

I don't need Thad Winchester. And I don't need a fling. I need a man who will give me security. Stability. A future. Financial well-being. A respected position in the community.

Her brain settled for a moment into a stunned silence.

Couldn't she get that anywhere? Even in Colorado?

Suddenly, she realized that's all she'd ever really wanted in life. A man to love her unconditionally. And it really didn't matter about the house on the east side. Could it be possible she could be just as happy with a ranch house in the Rockies?

But what about her job?

A tiny voice in her head reminded her that jobs in education were readily available most anywhere there were kids. Were there kids living in these mountains. Surely to goodness, there were kids.

But it really wasn't about Colorado vs. Kentucky, was it? It was about a whole lot more than that.

Her gaze settled on the camp through layers of pine boughs, catching a glimpse of Thad's back. Her fingertips tingled, remembering how smooth his skin felt there. How coarse the hairs on his chest were. How rough. Sensual. Primal. She brought her fingers to her lips. How wicked and stimulating his whiskers felt against her tender flesh.

Jerking her body alert, she sat up a little straighter. *C'mon, Kim. Get your priorities straight. Since when has Thad ever showed that he remotely desires sharing his ranch house with you? Especially when he just keeps walking away. When all he can do is give you a little peek of his potent sexuality, and then pull out like a scared adolescent boy.*

All right. I'm here and there's not a damn thing I can do about it. It doesn't matter how haywire my hormones get around Thad when he obviously doesn't want anything past a few minutes of groping. I'm going back to Kentucky. In one piece. Back to where I'm needed by my students and my family. Where my obligations outweigh this wacky situation Jillie has gotten me into.

I can't starve myself to death or I'll have no strength to carry my own body out of this godforsaken gulch. I'm going to make the best of this situation and then get the heck out of the mountains before I kill someone. Jillie. Thad. It doesn't matter. Just whoever crosses my path first.

* * *

While snatching a plate from the table next to the cookstove, Kim tossed a glance to the trio to her right. Engrossed in their meal, she ignored them as well and lifted a small portion of stew onto her plate. She added a piece of garlic toast, poured herself a cup of iced tea, and then sat beside Jillie as if it were the most natural thing in the world for her to do.

The only trouble was, sitting beside Jillie meant that she also had to sit directly opposite Thad.

For once, she concentrated solely on her meal. Never looking up. She was starved. Each of them ate in silence for about thirty seconds.

"Gee, it sure was a wonderful afternoon out there today, wasn't it, Mack?" Jillie placed her chin in her hands and struck a love-sick pose toward him.

"Oh, yeah. Blue skies. Green grass. Cool breezes. It was quite an afternoon." Mack gave Jillie a lazy grin, then nodded and slowly cast his gaze toward Kim.

She sneered back.

"How did you and Thad spend your afternoon?" Jillie inquired sweetly.

Kim's chin dropped as she turned toward her used-to-be friend. *I'm going to kill you, Jillie, Abernathy.*

"Maybe Thad and Kim want to keep their afternoon private, Jillie. Just between themselves."

You, too, asshole cowboy.

Ignore them, she told herself. She crossed and re-crossed her legs under the table, accidentally bumping Thad's knee as she did so. Electric charges lanced up her leg. Her gaze shot up. His zipped across the table. It was just a slight skittering of their gazes, but Kim was sure it struck an arc between them. Immediately, she cast her eyes downward and took up her fork.

Another moment of silence hovered over the foursome.

"Good stew, Kim."

Lifting her head, she glared in Mack's direction. "Thanks," Her reply was a bit curt.

"Yeah," Jillie intervened, nodding to Mack. "And the toast's really good, too."

Kim shrugged. "Toast is toast."

"No, I mean it," Jillie took another bite, chewing and talking. "It's the way you mixed the garlic with the butter and the way it browned so evenly around the edges. Perfect. Kim, you can really cook."

Kim put down her fork and looked Jillie straight in the eyes. "Are you insane?"

Jillie feigned surprise. "What?"

"Kim used to be a Home Economics teacher, did you know that, Thad? She taught cooking." Mack tossed in.

Confused at the jump in the conversation, Kim jerked her gaze back to Mack. He elbowed Thad in the side. Kim caught a glimpse of Thad's eyes as his gaze narrowly brushed hers then tried to tamp down the little thrill that raced over her spine as their eyes met.

"No." He cleared his throat, then took a drink of tea. "No, I didn't."

"She can really cook," Jillie interjected

Thad met Kim's eyes, head on. "I'll bet." She swallowed as his gaze seared hers. Was it suddenly getting hot out here? "I thought Sarah made the stew," he went on, finally.

"Actually, she didn't," Kim returned. "I had some free time." She deliberately stared into his eyes. "I made it from scratch. Sarah had planned another meal entirely. I improvised."

Thad's unmoving gaze penetrated hers. "You do that well —improvise."

"So I've been told." She picked up her toast and bit into it.

Thad held the connection for a few seconds more. "I'll bet."

Again, silence.

"But Kim's a guidance counselor now," Jillie interrupted. After a second, Thad broke away and resumed his eating. Kim felt her shoulders drop. "The kids just love her. She's so good with them."

Silence.

Kim took a bite of stew. It tasted like wallpaper paste.

"Oh, and did you all know that Kim helps sponsor the literary magazine at our high school in her spare time?" Jillie blurted out.

Where did that come from? She tossed a questioning glance at Jillie.

"Thad used to write for the school paper," Mack added.

"Sports," Thad threw in. "That hardly counts." He resumed eating.

"Oh, well, Kim would appreciate that. She used to be the editor of her college newspaper. And she was president of her sorority and is an officer in the Junior League and does volunteer work at a woman's crisis center in Lexington."

Mack chuckled. "Well, Thad's the only rancher I know who has subscriptions to both The Wall Street Journal and The New Yorker. Did I mention he's president of our local chapter of The Cattlemen's Association? And he used to volunteer down at the animal shelter before we got into the pack trip business."

What is this? Kim cast Jillie, and then Mack, a look of disbelief. "You two can quit with the mutual admiration society. It's not going anywhere."

"But Kim," Jillie interrupted. "We're just trying to get you two to see—"

"Forget it, Jill." This was embarrassing. And all Thad could do was stare into his stew. Damn him. Why won't he say something?

Thad cleared his throat. "Seems to me," he finally added, looking up and locking his gaze with Kim's, "that we're both fairly grounded in our own separate lives. That each of us are pretty set in our ways. Wouldn't you say that, Kim?"

Stunned, she stared at him. What did he want her to say? That she wasn't grounded? That she'd pack up and follow him anywhere? Well, that wasn't likely.

She dropped her chin in a nod. "I guess you could say that, Thad. My life has been pretty much mapped out for me since I was a toddler." After a lengthy moment, she finally dragged her gaze from his, ignoring the tightening in her chest. But it was difficult to ignore the tears filling her eyes. Hearing him say the words, and her verbalization of them, made the point hit entirely too close to home.

Sounded to her like it was all settled and decided.

Jillie drummed her fingers on the tabletop for a few irritating minutes. "You know, Kim? What really would be good right now is one of your cream pies."

Oh, hell. No more....

Jillie took her fork in her hand and pointed it at Thad, directing her conversation his way. "God, they're the best. Almost better than sex. Sinfully delicious. Especially the chocolate. I could just lick the very pan." She paused for a moment, then suddenly, her face became animated. "I know, Thad. Maybe when we get back to the ranch, Kim will make one for you. Then you can try a piece."

Thad's fork clanked to the table.

"Uh... I mean taste a little bit."

Kim choked on her tea.

"Sample the goods?"

She grabbed Jillie's thigh.

"Er...eat a slice?"

Kim pounded her fist on the table. *Bang. You're dead.* "Jillie, shut up!" Oh, God. She couldn't, wouldn't, be able to look Thad in the face again. "Have you lost your freakin' mind?"

"I'm only trying to help, Kim."

Kim threw up her hands in frustration. Tears threatened to spill over her lids. "Help? With what?" She picked up a plate and headed for the garbage container, leaving the rest of them behind. Immediately, she tossed the plate into the wash basin with a clank. "I'm not doing the damned dishes tonight. I quit! I think it's about time you two have a go at something other than each other!"

Kim headed for her tent, finally letting go of the tears. She'd been so damned angry the whole week, but she'd never allowed herself tears. Not until now. How dare Jillie and Mack treat her this way? And Thad! He didn't do one thing to stop them.

Could it be that the affirmation from him, that their lives were very separate and grounded was the thing that brought the tears on? She didn't want to think about it.

A firm hand grasped her forearm, urging her to stop and turn around.

"Kim," Thad's voice was soft, gentle. "Slow down there."

"Oh, God, Thad. Just leave me alone, all right?" She tried to jerk away.

"No, we need to talk."

Kim huffed out a breath and glanced skyward, then gulped in a sob. "Talk? We don't talk, Thad. All we do is argue."

"I know that." He pulled her closer, his hands encircling both her wrists. "I know. It's my fault." Reaching out, he brushed a line of tears from her cheek. She shivered at his touch, but couldn't tear her gaze away from his face.

"I don't understand you, Thad Winchester," she whispered. "One minute you're yelling at me and the next you're comforting me, like when I was sick. One minute I think you want to kiss me and the next you're high-tailing away from me so fast it makes me dizzy."

"I know."

"Why?"

He rubbed his hands up and down her arms. "Because I'm attracted to you, Kim."

She snorted and tried to smile. "And that's a problem?"

She knew it was. He tugged her closer. She peered into the deep depths of his eyes. "Are you attracted to me?" he murmured. She tried to remember that he avoided answering her question.

But she melted against him, anyway. She could only nod.

"What do you want from me, Kim?" His lips were heading dangerously close to hers.

She hesitated. "What I want, Thad, is for you to kiss me and hold me and not walk away."

The warmth of his breath against her lips sent Kim spiraling. His arms encircled her body. The heat emanating from him warmed her to her very center. Then his lips brushed hers, ever so gently.

"For how many days, Kim?" he breathed. "How long do you want me to kiss and hold you?"

"How many days do we have left?" she queried softly.

"Not nearly enough." The rough stubble of his chin grazed hers. Kim caught her breath as he grasped her even closer. Then briefly, he drew back and stared into her face.

It was then she knew. He expected her to go home. Whatever they shared in these mountains together would be left here. He'd go back to his ranch. She'd go back to her students.

And life as they knew it, would simply go on.

Suddenly, she knew that wasn't enough. She wanted more than that.

She wrenched herself out of his grasp and stepped backwards a few steps. "Goodnight, Thad," she whispered. "I'll see you in the morning."

* * *

Thad knew he was black and blue all over from tossing and turning on the damned cold ground for the past two hours. Not even the cushion of the sleeping bag helped. There were too many rocks and roots protruding up from underneath.

He hadn't really taken the time to investigate where he'd tossed the thing earlier. All he'd known at the time was that he needed to get away from camp, from Mack and that irritating Jillie—and from Kim.

He needed wide open spaces.

There was no way he'd stay cooped up in that blasted dome tent until morning. He needed air. Needed to breathe. So, after he figured the rest of them were down for the night, he'd rolled up his sleeping bag and took off into the mountain behind them. A bit off the trail, but safe enough, he found a small clearing where he could easily view the night's scenery and lay back to watch the heavens at the same time.

Finally, he grew still and studied the night sky.

The stars winked at him like dainty diamonds against black velvet. Delicate. Sparkling. Yet strong and powerful. Almost seductive.

Like Kim.

"Damn."

He'd never met a woman like her.

Kim was different.

She really had never been charming. He was glad, he'd always hated fake attitudes in women. She hadn't put on airs around any of them. Kim had simply been herself.

And she wasn't witty, trying to vie for everyone's attention. Just pointed.

And she dared to buck him. Had a little spirit.

Kim was honest. He could see it in her eyes, in every expression on her face. She'd let her true feelings be known more than once. She'd failed to rein in her passions from the beginning. There was nothing fake about what they'd shared this afternoon.

But he'd walked away from her. Not once, but twice. And all because of some stupid notion that business and pleasure should never be mixed.

And how stupid a notion was that? Maybe Mack was right. Was this an official pack trip now that it was just the four of them?

It was if he was taking their money.

"Damn."

Thad closed his eyes and the image of Kim standing in the stream came to him. Against the black of his eyelids, he played the scene out again.

His hands on her breasts. The taste of her skin. The scent of roses in her hair.

She'd dared him to come to her. She'd invited him with her eyes. She'd tempted him with her fingers sliding over her skin. Was losing a few bucks worth losing something that could be even more lasting? Like loving Kim?

Thad snapped his eyes open and sat up. Loving Kim? She had intended to give herself to him. Freely. Damn the consequences. Damn the differences in their lifestyles. Damn the fact that they lived thousands of miles apart.

And damn the fact that they both were hesitant to get involved.

She would have given herself to him.

Freely.

Money be damned. There were a lot more important things to be considered here.

A branch snapped about twenty feet below and Thad jerked to attention and froze. Listening. Elk? A bear? He had seen no signs of bears the past few days, but it wouldn't be uncommon. That they had food stored away sometimes triggered a visit.

He was always careful, burning the garbage and washing out any used food cans, but one could never be sure.

A rustle sounded in the trees. Closer. He heard a small shriek. Then a thin beam of light bobbled up through the trees and disappeared.

Chapter Twelve

"Oh...hell's bells," Kim whispered. She winced as she stretched to rub at her right ankle." What did I do, take a wrong turn?"

Glancing about her, she reached for the flashlight, which had been knocked out of her hand as she'd tripped over a knotty tree root. "Stupid trees. I thought roots were supposed to grow straight down into the ground."

Sitting here muttering to herself certainly wasn't helping the situation.

If only she hadn't needed to pee. Of course, it was the middle of the night, that's when it always happens. There was no way she could wait until morning. And besides, the tent was stuffy, and she needed some air. So, she'd picked up the flashlight and ventured into the trees.

She just hadn't planned on getting a bit discombobulated on her return trip.

Or twisting her ankle on uncooperative roots.

The flashlight sent out a weakening beam against the trees in front of her. She played it over the area trying to figure out exactly which way the camp was situated. But as she searched, the beam slowly, but surely, faded away into nothing.

She shook the thing. It blinked on for a second, then plunged her back into total darkness.

The batteries were dead. A lancing sensation of fear shot through her abdomen.

"C'mon. Give me a break." She rolled her eyes toward the heavens.

In total darkness, she assessed the situation as she saw it. She was lost. It was after midnight. Her ankle was tender. Camp was not far away, if she only knew which direction to head. Someone had obviously failed to leave a lantern on in the dining fly...she could probably thank Jillie and Mack for that. It was chilly out and she'd slipped on only a thin cotton shirt and her blue jeans. And she had no light.

It was going to be a long night.

The best thing she figured she could do for herself was to stay put for the next few hours. At morning's light, she could easily see what direction to go, then she could make her way back to camp before anyone realized she'd been stupid enough to lose herself in the woods during the middle of the night.

Well, at least it was a plan.

Behind her, something rustled. And was that a...grunt?

A shot of adrenaline traveled from her stomach to her throat.

Or she could run. Screaming.

The rustling grew closer. Out of sheer fear, Kim picked up the useless flashlight and hurled it into the trees.

It landed somewhere with a thud. The rustling stopped.

Now, plan two seemed the better option. Even with a sore ankle.

A twig snapped. Something moved in the trees again and she froze. Wild animal? A rabbit? Deer? Elk?

Oh, God, a bear?

It was all she could do to keep her teeth from chattering. Finally, she stuck her lower lip between her teeth and bit it, hard, just to keep her teeth from rattling and attracting whatever was out there to her location.

Her heart pounded erratically. And with each wayward beat, her breathing echoed the thundering pulse in her ears.

She prayed that if she sat perfectly still, whatever it was would pass right by without noticing her there.

That's when she thought about smelling.

Don't wild animals possess a keen sense of smell? They could smell human scent, right? And didn't the human scent signal...danger to them? And wouldn't they sometimes attack when approached with a dangerous situation?

A heavy thud sounded too close to her ear. She leaned back against a tree and closed her eyes tight, hugging her shivering body. And prayed.

The deafening silence that followed was too much for her to handle. Where was the beast? Was he assessing her? Trying to decide if she was good enough to eat? If he wanted to take her home to his family for a midnight snack? What the hell was the animal waiting for?

She opened her eyes. Slowly.

And realized she was caught in a beam of light.

Squinting, she brought a hand up to her eyes. Unless a bear could hold a flashlight, she was feeling a bit safer.

"Kim?" His voice sounded just a tad bit defeated.

"Uh, yeah."

"What are you doing out here, in the middle of the night? Alone."

After that split-second of relief, followed one of agitation, then another of thanking God for answered prayers. When her eyes finally adjusted to the light, she stood up to Thad.

"At the moment, I haven't the vaguest idea."

Thad lowered the flashlight. "Are you lost?"

"I guess you could say that."

"What were you doing out here?"

"Do I really have to explain? This is embarrassing enough."

Kim glanced off to her left and Thad didn't answer for a minute. *He thinks you're a complete idiot.*

"No. You don't."

Thank you.

He stepped closer and Kim turned to look at him. Even in the dark, she could see his face. She guessed her eyes had adjusted to the lack of light, and it helped that the stars had lent a subtle radiance to the surrounding atmosphere. With the muted and still weakening beam of the flashlight, he looked softer. His hat was gone, which showed the gray streaks at his temples against the black night. His chiseled features seemed more relaxed than she'd ever seen, the harshness gone from his face.

He looked almost...tender.

Before she knew it, he'd reached out and grasped her hand. "C'mon, let's get out of here before this light gives way altogether."

He led the way. Kim's hand tingled. They felt so small wrapped up with his big fingers. His skin felt rough and callused, a working man's hand. Full of character. Texture. Definition. Strength. Just like Thad.

She realized she preferred holding that kind of hand.

It wasn't long before they were out of the trees and the stars burst forth in the sky above them. Thad led her a little further, then stopped. He didn't let go of her hand.

She looked into the sky, and then glanced around her.

"This isn't the way to the camp, is it?" She turned toward him.

He looked down, searching her eyes. "No. It's not." Still holding her hand, he led her to a flatter area. "Want to sit a minute before we go back? I've got a sleeping bag over here."

Tentatively, she sat and waited for him to sit beside her. For a while, they sat in silence, staring into the night sky. The only movement between the two of them was Thad's caressing of Kim's hand. With each stroke, Kim felt her heart pick up a quicker cadence. She lowered her gaze to their hands and watched his fingers tenderly glide over hers. She couldn't help but wonder about the turnabout of his actions. He seemed almost...happy to see her.

"So, what were you doing up here?" she asked him.

"Couldn't sleep. Too much stuff messing around in my head." She watched his profile silhouetted against a moonbeam.

She risked a grin. "I know. That tent is just too small. I was bouncing off the walls."

He nodded his agreement.

"You know," he began after a moment, "you and I really need to talk." He faced her. His eyes were so dark, she thought she could see the stars in them. "We got off on the wrong foot."

Kim pushed out a thin breath. "I'm pretty bullheaded, sometimes."

The corner of his mouth curled into a smile. And she liked the way he smiled.

"Bullheaded isn't even close to the word I'd use to describe myself," he added.

"I think it's safe to say that we're both pretty stubborn."

Thad laughed, but after a moment, his face grew serious. "I thought you were going to be such a nuisance."

"I guess I was."

"Actually, you surprised the hell out of me."

"Really?" Kim straightened her back and edged a little closer.

His gaze dropped to their hands. "You're learning how to handle the horse. The food's been great. You've done every task I've asked you to do."

"And that surprised you?"

"Like a shot out of the blue."

"Why?"

Thad paused. "I... I don't know. It just didn't seem like you were cut out for this sort of thing."

She cringed. "What do you mean, this sort of thing? The pack trip? Or being with you?"

He grimaced a little and shook his head. "The terrain is pretty rugged and considering the way you handled the trail ride. I wasn't quite sure..."

Kim breathed a sigh of relief. She wasn't quite sure what he was going to say.

"Anyway, I was dead wrong. You're a lot stronger than I thought you were. You can probably handle just about anything life would care to throw at you."

Somehow, Kim wasn't sure he was talking about the pack trip, now. Amazed at his assessment of her, Kim put her other hand next to his and stared at the stark difference in the two. They were together. Almost as one unit. And it was beautiful. Could they have a chance? "There are some moments when I'm a lot stronger than others. I guess I've called upon some basic instincts this week. I know it wasn't very flattering."

He chuckled. "Hell, I wasn't exactly going overboard to play the gracious host, myself." He paused for a minute and Kim watched his profile. "You know, Kim, I have this rule."

"Rule?"

"Yeah." He turned and faced her. She met his gaze. Cautiously, he reached up and trailed a soft finger along her cheek. "It's a rule about never mixing business with pleasure. About keeping all guest relationships strictly professional."

"In other words," Kim added, "you don't usually warm all your female guests' sleeping bags for them?"

A slow grin broke his face. He just stared at her, peering into her eyes. "No, Kim," he whispered. "It's not usually part of the package deal."

"Good."

He was so close. His lips only centimeters away; his breath warm and coffee-laced, moist against her skin. "You know," she whispered, "I used to think cowboys were nothing but roping and riding ranch rogues. And I didn't figure there was any place for a woman like me with a man like you. No matter how much I was attracted."

That lifted his hooded gaze. "Kim..." His voice caressed. "I never dreamed you'd be attracted to me."

"I never wanted to be," she admitted, searching his face. "It was just something I couldn't help."

"I know how that feels." He held her gaze for a moment. "Kim, this afternoon I wanted you more than I've ever wanted a woman. I don't know why I left you like that. It was the most frustrating experience I've ever had. Can you forgive me?"

His thumb brushed over her upper lip, and her breathing quickened. She watched his eyes as he followed the trail of his thumb caressing her cheek and jaw and chin. His touches were pure heaven and with each stroke, she felt her desire let go a little more, and more, until her breathing was more labored than quickened.

His fingertips caressed the tiny nerve endings of her face, causing a slow torture to build deep inside her.

"Thad Winchester," she whispered, while lifting her hand to his chin, "Don't you dare walk away from me this time."

His eyes flashed and Kim knew they were at a point of no return. Slowly, he shook his head, his eyes never leaving her face. "I couldn't walk away even if I wanted."

His lips descended and just as they touched, she whispered, "Good. Because I'm not about to let you go."

More gently than she'd ever realized he could be, Thad slid his hand down Kim's neck and laid it flat against her chest. While his lips caressed hers in a slow, lazy rhythm, she pushed closer into his embrace.

"Your heart's beating so fast," he whispered as he drew away from her lips and began a trail of kisses down her throat toward her heart.

She placed her hand on his chest. "Mine's not the only one," she whispered back.

"No," he breathed. "It's not."

Thad's fingers groped for the placket of Kim's shirt, and began a slow descent, unfastening each as he nibbled and suckled on her neck, at her collarbone. She arched into him and felt the chilly air hit her erect, bare nipples, as he opened her shirt and slipped it over her shoulders.

Thad drew back and looked at her.

She opened her eyes. His looking at her, her breasts bared to the cool night air, under the starlit sky, made her feel exhilarated and quite sexy—and only stimulated her arousal.

"God, you are beautiful."

Humbly, he cupped a breast. Kim's chest lifted in heated breath. She watched as he gently explored each mound of her flesh, his dark, rough fingers grazing over her nipples, underneath, around, and then finally taking both hands and lifting her breasts into his palms, squeezing, tempting.

She loved the electrifying sensations driving up within her from watching both his face as he fondled her, and feeling his methodical, tortuous, but gentle assault of her breasts. She slipped the shirt completely off her shoulders and arms and reached out to grasp the buttons of his.

In the next instant, Thad laid her back against the sleeping bag. One hand still held and teased a breast; his lips and tongue ravished her mouth. His tongue, wet and moist encircled her lips and gently played with hers, urging them both into a frenzied passion. Kim pulled and tugged at his clothing.

The second she'd freed him of his shirt, her hands went to his broad, muscled chest. Remembering how good he felt beneath her palms, she sighed and smoothed her hands over him like a crazed woman, desiring the touch, the feel, of his flesh in her hands.

Thad angled himself over her and Kim stroked her fingers through his hair as he peered down. He took quick, wet kisses from her as he watched her face, as though studying every feature, every freckle, every nuance there. Watching him, filled with desire and pleasure, Kim felt such a closeness, a bond, and a oneness envelope her. There were only two people in the world tonight who mattered. And that was she and Thad.

He spoke in a hushed whisper. "I can't believe you're here with me, Kimmy." His hands framed her face and he continued to stare into her eyes. "I'm not sure if I've ever felt what I'm feeling now."

She silenced him with a finger to his lips. "Shush...." she breathed. "Right now, there's nothing in the world that matters."

"But what about later?"

A slight panic grabbed her, but she ignored it. Tracing his lip with her fingertip, she watched as Thad's lips parted and he drew her finger inside and sucked. She held her finger there, absorbing the rough texture of his tongue and growing more aroused by the moment. "Later will take care of itself. Love me, Thad."

He embraced her with his head on her chest, as if he couldn't bear to think of what later might bring.

Gasping a quick breath, Thad fumbled with the snap of her jeans and hurriedly lowered her zipper.

She wanted him to take her. Slowly. Quickly. It didn't matter. She was dying to have him inside her.

In the next instant Thad slipped his hands around her hips and removed both blue jeans and panties in one swift motion. She lay there, her body bared to the twinkling night sky and Thad's ardent gaze. For the longest time, it seemed, he simply stared, lying beside him, while she smoothed her palm over his chest and belly, occasionally dipping slightly beneath the waistband of his jeans.

Thad's raking gaze almost sent her into tremors without so much as a touch. The open skies, the night breezes kissing her heated skin, her pebbled nipples, her moist and heated center, all gave way to a wild abandonment she'd never experienced.

Then he touched her. One finger gently grazed a hip bone and began a lazy ascent toward her belly, circling her navel, then traveling upward to a flushed nipple. Again, he circled and teased the dusky pink until he'd raised the gooseflesh all over her body. All the while, their eyes remained connected in a sizzling embrace, and Kim's breathing quickened to panting.

"You're driving me crazy," she whispered, leaning closer to touch her lips to his.

"I'm savoring every second," he whispered back. "And showing you how unselfish this cowboy can be." He nipped her lower lip with his teeth, pulled her closer, and growled. The finger that was still sending swirls of sensation across her breasts was now beginning a leisurely descent toward her belly, and lower.

Kim moaned and grasped at Thad's chest as he continued his unhurried quest to reach her center. Again, he lazily circled her delicate mound and threaded his fingers through her dark curls. She sucked in one quick breath after another as every pleasured nerve ending between her legs cried out to be touched.

"Oh... Thad." She rose and nuzzled his neck, urging her body closer to his. "What are you doing to me?"

He pulled away and she caught the wicked grin that flashed over his face. Then lower, she felt him cup her, more firmly now —and took her mouth in a heated kiss as he slowly massaged her aching flesh.

He stroked her, setting out on a course of slow, tortuous pleasure as the essence of an igniting fire built deep within her. His tongue delved into her mouth. Kim took him in, hungrily sucking. His fingers probed and opened, his palm pressed against her, circling, rubbing. Filled with him, she clutched at his belly and grasped his flesh above his waistband, wanting so much more than that in her hands. Reaching, she wanted to touch him, wanted his throbbing need in her hands.

Together, they rid him of his jeans and boots. Thad urgently kicked them away from the sleeping bag. She reached for him, and Kim gazed at the chiseled structure of his body in the moonlight.

He was beautiful.

And then his finger touched her swollen cleft, playing, flicking, tantalizing her, until the banked fire within erupted into flames that licked high into her inner core.

She bucked against his hand at the explosion, wanting to feel him holding her there until all sensation was spent. He held her body close, her head against his beating heart; her arms wrapped around him. And when her labored breathing slowed to a mere pant, Thad gently massaged her aching flesh until her tremors subsided.

Still holding her close, he shifted so his body was over hers and Kim, her eyes still closed, relished in the warmth of him draped over her. His hands framed her face.

"Kimmy," he whispered, "look at me."

Opening her eyes, she looked into the face of a man who

looked like he'd just been given the world. He peered deep into her eyes as his thumbs rubbed feather-like circles at her temples.

"I want to look into your eyes. I want to see the passion I put on your face...before I lose control." She opened her lips to speak, but he silenced her with a tender kiss.

His hardened shaft probed, then entered her with one quick thrust. Thad froze over her, stilled in what she hoped was pure pleasure. It was like she'd swallowed him. He'd filled her completely and fully. She grasped him and as she looked up, his face pointed to the sky, his eyes shut tight. She placed a hand on his cheek.

Thad lowered his body against hers and nuzzled her lips, her neck, as his lower body thrust again and again into her, at first like a slow, methodical waltz, then crescendoing into a frenzied rhapsody. Kim took him in, met his thrusts, feeling his heat from the inside, building until again, the inferno burned within her. And just when she thought she couldn't stand the increasing fervor a second longer, she burst into a thousand sparkling embered notes, his name a pianissimo whisper on her lips.

She clawed at Thad, pulling him closer. He firmly thrust again and once more, then moaned her name over and over as he held her hips steady and exploded inside her with one last quivering thrust. She felt his urgent throbbing against her tender insides; a trembling passed through him as he collapsed over her and held her tight against him.

And as Kim held him, her hands softly stroking his back, savoring the feel of him inside her, his flesh against and within hers, it was difficult for her to hold back the tears.

* * *

Moments later, Kim lay in the crook of Thad's shoulder, her cheek resting against his chest and both their arms wrapped around each other. Deep in the sleeping bag, their legs interlocked. A sleepy, wonderful aura surrounded them. Tender touches and hushed whispered filled the night.

"Shouldn't we be getting back to camp?" she whispered, nuzzling closer into Thad's chest.

She felt him shake his head no and gather her closer. "I never want to leave here," he returned. "I've never felt so close to anyone in my life."

His voice was almost a croak. Kim lifted herself up on one elbow to look into his face but caught just a glimpse of his closed eyes before he stopped her by rolling onto his side and pulling her deeper into the sleeping bag.

"Don't move. I'm afraid we'll break the spell. Stay close. I need you close." He was almost pleading.

A tremor spiked up within her, settling around her heart. He needed her?

Burrowing closer, she positioned herself where she could see his face. Content and calm were the only two words she could think of to describe how he looked. She wondered how she looked to him?

"I need you, too, Thad," she whispered.

A hand clasped her head against his chest; his fingers stoked her scalp with gentle motion. His arms held her close. "Sleep," he urged her, his voice a faint murmur. "I'll keep you safe. Stay with me, my Kimmy. Sleep."

Chapter Thirteen

"Wake up, sleepyhead."

Kim groaned and stretched, then burrowed further into Thad's warmth. She knew exactly where she was and all that had transpired the night before. And she didn't want to move one inch.

"I don't wanna."

Thad moved and positioned himself above her. Kim threw the back of her hand over her mouth and yawned. Slowly, she opened her eyes. The sun just rising spread a marbled gray and pink stain across the sky. Thad's wonderful face stared back at her.

"Mornin'," she whispered.

His hands framed her face; his fingers made feather-like strokes across her cheeks as he gazed into her eyes.

"It wasn't a dream," he whispered.

She smiled. "No, it wasn't." She studied him, then a momentary panic settled inside her. "Is everything...are you...okay?"

"Perfect." He lightly kissed her lips and Kim mentally sighed. "Isn't it?" he added, tentatively.

She arched up to meet his kiss, nibbled his lower lip, and then swiped her tongue across his mustache. "Um. Yes," she breathed. "Your mustache tickles."

Thad drew back in surprise. "Oh, it does, does it?"

"It does."

"You like it?"

"Very much."

"Where do you like it best?"

She felt her eyes widen. "I'm—I'm not sure."

Thad arched a brow and an evil expression passed over his face. A second later, he was kissing her, rubbing his mustache over her lips and face. "You like it there."

Kim giggled. "Uh-huh."

Playfully, he slid lower into the sleeping bag, pulling the zipper down to allow him easier access. His mouth and mustache made a trail down to her breasts. She moaned when he took one nipple after the other inside his mouth, taking care to brush her delicate nipples periodically with the coarse hair over his lip.

"And what about here?" His hoarse whisper came from within the sleeping bag.

"Uh-huh, there too."

And then he slid lower.

"Thad, no," she breathed. "The sun's almost up. Someone... oh, uh-huh...yeah—" She felt the prickle of his mustache against her inner thigh. "Someone could come by." She managed to say the entire sentence in one quick breath.

"They've already come and gone. What about here?"

He opened her cleft and brushed his lips and mustache across her tender, swollen nub. "Wha— Who? Ahh, yeah... there, too."

She was definitely a goner.

Several breathless minutes later they mutually, as well as reluctantly, decided it was time to dress and head back to the camp.

She clasped Thad's hand and nuzzled him as they descended the small rise behind the camp. "Selfish is definitely not a word in your vocabulary, is it?" she asked, peering up into his face, teasing.

Thad stopped and then after a long, thorough look, reached down to kiss the tip of her nose. "I aim to please, ma'am."

"You please very well, sir." She gave him a sly grin.

"Thank you."

They walked in silence for a few more minutes. The smell of sausage frying tickled her nose. They were getting closer to camp.

"What are we going to tell Jillie and Mack when they see us...together?" she inquired.

Thad stared straight ahead. "We don't have to tell them anything. They already know."

"What?" Kim stopped and turned.

"They were sneaking around looking for us early this morning. That's what woke me."

"And did you talk to them?"

"No, they ran off. They didn't know I was awake."

"I'm never going to hear the end of it. You have no idea how overbearing Jillie can be."

Thad looked at her and grinned. "I've noticed. Brace yourself. We're here. And there they are."

Kim turned. In front of her stood Jillie, a broad smile stretched across her face. Her arms were crossed and she held a spatula in one hand. Mack stood at her side with his arm draped around her shoulders. A glance at his face revealed the same smirk.

"Well-well-well, the little lost lamb returns with the big, gruff wolf. What do you think, Mack? Do you think she cried wolf all night? Think he huffed and puffed, and—my, what is it big, bad wolves do to little lambs anyway, eat them alive?"

Mack snickered.

"Can it, Jill," Kim interrupted. "We've all got the picture, so you can stop now." She wasn't about to tell Jillie or anyone else about how bad her big, gruff wolf had been last night. The little lamb, too.

Jillie flashed her silly grin. "Okay. Anyone up to..." she flashed the spatula in the air, "breakfast? I know I'm ravished. What about the two of you?"

Kim sighed and threw Thad a helpless grin. "Yeah, I'll help. Lead the way."

There was no besting Jillie when she was on a roll.

* * *

The metal cup of coffee warmed his hands as Thad stood a bit removed from the scene, leaning against a tree near where they had picketed the horses and mules. He listened to Kim laughing with Jillie as they bantered back and forth while preparing breakfast. He watched Kim. Her actions were infinitely more confident that a few days earlier. More relaxed.

She looked, and acted, happy to be exactly where she was. Thad smiled. He liked her here. Could she be happy with a life like this? His life was no picnic, that was sure. Compared to what he imagined her life was like, this could only get dull and monotonous after a time. She might think it exciting for a while, but what if she grew to hate it? Hate him for wanting her here? He couldn't stand that.

It was damned difficult to admit, but she added spice to the camp, to his life, and he wasn't sure he ever wanted to give that up.

But he couldn't ever be sure of what she wanted, could he? Could he risk taking her into his life only to find she'd become bored over time? And it seemed, although they'd not talked about it, that she had a life waiting for her back in Kentucky. A job, which she obviously was good at. A family. And even though he was extremely attracted to her, felt almost lost in her, he really didn't know her well enough to guess at what her reaction would be about leaving all those things behind.

Would she ever consider...?

There were things they'd not discussed, probably hadn't even thought of, that were going to need their attention at some point. Soon. He did not know how he was going to broach the subject. Or if she would. But it was imminent that they would have to discuss what will happen when the trip was over. It was something he didn't care to think about now. It was the first time in a long time that he wasn't ready to get back to the ranch.

"So, you finally bit the bullet, eh?"

Mack stepped beside him, jarring his thoughts; Thad kept his gaze on Kim.

"You might say that." He lifted the coffee cup to his lips and took a sip, feeling Mack's gaze on him. Finally, he turned to his friend. "Look, Mack. I know I've been a little short with you lately."

Mack shook his head. "Forget it. What worries me now is what's going to happen when she leaves."

Thad tried not to show the flash of panic that stabbed his heart at Mack's words. "When she leaves, I'll deal with it." He couldn't fathom the possibility. Not yet. It was too soon. Even if he knew it was bound to happen.

Mack studied him. "And then you're going to be hell to live

with for the next twenty years or so." He paused for a minute and Thad turned his attention back to Kim. "Do you love her?"

After a second's hesitation, Thad broke his gaze and tossed the rest of his coffee onto the grass. Then he looked Mack straight in the eyes. "Love? I care for her, maybe a little too much, but it's too soon to talk about love. Let's just see what happens, all right?"

Mack let the still silence fall between them. Thad leaned back against the tree, hoping that he would take the hint and decide to drop the subject. It was hell enough to discuss all the options in his own mind, he wasn't ready to verbalize his thoughts. He'd waited forty years for the right woman to come along. In forty years, not one had tempted him to this degree. Could he convince her that life would be worth living here in Colorado? With him?

"Thad, she's good for you. Don't let her get away. Do whatever you can to keep her. I don't think you'll regret it."

Thad glanced at the ground and shook his head. "You don't understand, do you?" After a second's wait, he lifted his face to look at Mack. "If I had my way, I'd hog-tie her and keep her in my bed morning, noon, and night. But I can't do that, Mack. I can't ask her to stay. I can't force her to stay if that's not what she wants."

"And how do you know she doesn't want that?"

"I don't. I guess I'm just preparing myself for the worst. The inevitable."

"I think you're waving the white flag a little too soon, here."

"I think it's too soon for us to speculate about any of this. She's got a life, Mack, and it doesn't include me."

"Why are you so all-fire sure she doesn't want you in it?"

Thad jerked his gaze back to the dining fly. Kim and Jillie were waving to them. That was exactly what he had to figure out. Kim Martin had seeped under his skin. He loved her. And it scared the living hell out of him that she wouldn't love him back.

He cleared his throat. "I think breakfast is ready." He started off.

Mack stepped beside him and they silently headed toward the camp.

As they approached the women, Thad forced any negativity out of his head. Breakfast was already on the table and as Kim smiled and patted the bench next to her, he slid in and pulled her to him, as though he needed to feel her next to him to prove that she was really there. And that she wanted him.

He placed a quick kiss on her cheek and relished in the smell of her hair, her skin, and inhaled deeply to keep her scent inside his lungs for as long as possible. *Damn, Kim, I'll go crazy without you, please don't leave me.*

Then he released her and realized both Jillie and Mack were staring at him.

"Better eat," he threw out in his old, gruff voice. "It's getting cold."

Jillie arched a brow. "Forgive me for staring, Thad, it's just that—"

"Shut up, Jillie." Mack nudged her in the side. She tossed a quick, puzzled glance his way, took in his warning look, and then nodded. After a moment, she picked up her fork and started eating.

"Well, that's a first." Kim reached for the salt and pepper and grinned across the table. Thad sensed it was an attempt to lighten up what had the potential of being a tense moment. "I've never been able to shut her up that easily, Mack. You must have some kind of powerful secret."

Jillie's elbow popped Mack in the side. "If you say one word, cowboy," she warned, "you are a dead man."

Mack's surprised face caught everyone off guard, then the

entire group exploded into laughter. Thad felt his shoulder and neck muscles drop into a more relaxed position as he let the laughter momentarily wash away his worries. He decided right then and there that he couldn't fret about what was going to happen at the end of the trip, what he needed to do was concentrate on making Kim happy today. The only way to play this game was to take it one step at a time. And every step along the way was just as important as the next one.

And if the days fell into place without a hitch, then maybe she'd decide on her own to be a part of his life, forever. And that's what it would have to be, her decision.

"So," Mack's voice interrupted his thoughts, "are we still heading out today?"

Thad stared across the table at Jillie, who stopped chewing her sausage in mid-bite. His gaze slid to Mack, and then he sidled a glance at Kim, whose startled face reflected a bit of fear back at him.

"No," he said in a low voice, watching Kim's face melt. "We'll keep the original schedule." He paused for a moment, the same melancholy feelings from earlier returning, difficult for him to shake. "I'm not ready to push out of here yet."

Kim's lips parted slightly, and he watched her tongue flick away a crumb of biscuit from her lip. "Good," she said softly. "That's real good."

* * *

A fine gray mist settled over the trail two days later as she rode quietly behind Thad. The two days had been filled with lazy mornings, afternoons exploring the mountains and even the Fremont expedition site, and nights filled with endless lovemaking. Kim had grown to crave Thad's touch, the warmth of his body, the scent of his skin. They'd become inseparable. The only thing that put a hint of a damper on their togetherness, was her imminent departure. They never discussed it. The days were like a fairy-tale and she hadn't wanted to burst the fantasy bubble. She refused to talk about leaving him. She knew it had to be done, but it was a thought she kept pushing further back into her brain.

The rushing waters of the waterfall had filled her ears for some time, so she'd anticipated its presence for a while, but nothing had prepared for the spectacular sight as Thad's horse, then hers, broke into a clearing.

Tiny stones and larger rocks and boulders, tumbled and smoothed by the rushing waters of time, bordered the edge of the mountain creek. Pooled into a deep hole, which looked perfect for fishing or swimming. Water spewed off the mountain, cascading into the cradle of rock, creating a picture-perfect scene for any photographer.

Kim walked Sunshine next to Thad's horse. "I wish I'd brought my camera," she whispered. "This is incredible."

It was difficult to pull her gaze away from the sight, but she did, feeling Thad staring at her. "I can bring you back anytime you want," he softly returned.

Kim searched his serious face. *Will there be a next time?* it seemed to ask. "I would like that."

His stony facade broke into a slight grin. Kim was relieved. It was a mystery what was going on in that man's head. One minute he was carefree as a bird, the next, stone-faced as a statue. And each time he looked at her like he was memorizing every nuance of her face, her heart tripped a beat, and she was a little frightened.

Thad dismounted and reached up to help her off her horse. "There's a great lookout over here, if you care to climb a little."

She nodded. "Okay."

He took her hand in his and led her away from the pooled water and up a small rocky incline. After a while, he dropped her hand so they could each gain balance to maneuver around the boulders and rocks jutting out from the mountain. It wasn't too hard a climb, but when they reached the top, she was glad for a breather.

Thad pulled her up the last few feet.

She smiled. "Whew! That was a little climb!"

"Yeah, but it's worth it. See." He pulled her into his side and pointed her away from the mountain.

Kim gasped. "Oh, my. It's breathtaking."

A panoramic vista of mountain and mist held her speechless. Craggy bare mountains in the distance contrasted with lush forests of assorted conifers and pines dipping into the valleys closer to them. The water rushing over the waterfall behind them fell into the creek meandering below, over rugged beds of rocks and boulders. White water cascades of smaller streams emptied into the larger creek, all on their way to unknown rivers, tumbling into canyons cut deep into the mountains. To their left, probably a mile or so away, there appeared to be a small lake.

Closer, were mountainside and patches of wildflowers. Beautiful, colorful, wildflowers.

"Oh, Thad," she whispered. "There are so many of them. What are they?" Lavenders, scarlets, and yellows dotted the landscape like an artist's palette.

Behind her now, Thad encircled her with his arms and held her close to his chest. He bent to whisper in her ear, his breath softly tickling her neck. "I don't know all of them. The tall red ones are Indian Paintbrush. The smaller scarlet ones, near the edge of the creek are primrose. And the lavender and white are Colorado Columbine."

"They're gorgeous." She turned in his arms and circled his neck, then reached up to plant a soft kiss on his lips. "Thank you for bringing me here. Can we get a closer look at those flowers before we leave?"

"Sure can. As I said, ma'am, I'm just aimin' to please."

Smiling, Kim settled back into him and clasped her hands over his arms. She didn't know when she'd felt this content, or happy. "Tell me where we are."

For a moment, Thad stood transfixed, looking out over the mountain range.

"You're looking at the western edge of the San Juan Mountains, just east of the Continental Divide," he began. "We'll end up due west of here," he pointed in that direction, "and descend down the mountains on the west side of the Divide as we head toward Elk Park. All the streams and creeks below us are falling east and will eventually end up in the Rio Grande." He paused for a moment. Kim tipped her head sideways to see his face. His eyes grazed the horizon. "I can't see any markers at the moment, but along there somewhere," again he pointed, "is the Colorado Trail. There are rock cairns occasionally, marking the trail."

Kim turned to face him. "The Colorado Trail?"

"It's a hiking trail. Starts around Denver, ends in Durango. About 470 miles long, if I remember correctly. Sometimes we'll see hikers when we head toward Elk Park to catch the spur. A lot of times they'll start or stop there, if they're out for a day or two hike."

"Wow, do people actually hike the entire distance?"

"Some do, I'm told. I'd rather ride." Thad framed her face with his hands. "So what do you think of...my little corner of the world?"

"I like it very much." There seemed to be a momentary relaxing of Thad's face when she answered.

"Is it much different from Kentucky?"

Kentucky was a universe away. "Yes. Very much different."

"Tell me." His eyes were hard again, penetrating deep into hers. Somehow, she wasn't sure he was talking about terrain. "Tell me all about Kim Martin and what she does in Kentucky."

She held his gaze for a moment, wondering what mysteries laid beyond those dark eyes of his. "Can we stay here for a while and talk?"

Thad wrapped her closer into his embrace. "We've got all day."

Settling down onto the rock, they leaned against an enormous boulder. Kim sighed. Thad kept his arms tight around her as she sat between his legs, her back leaning against his chest. She needed this—this closeness with Thad. Sharing. The togetherness. There was nothing and no one else to be considered. No Jillie and Mack. Not her mother's expectations. No student's problems crowding her mind.

There was only Thad. And it felt so good.

"Jillie and I share an apartment back home in Lexington."

Thad slid one hand between the snaps of her shirt, his warm palm caressing the skin just beneath her breasts. "I gathered that much."

"We went to school together since grade school but went off to different colleges. About five years ago Jillie was hired as a Biology teacher at my high school, and we reconnected. At that time, I was teaching Home Economics, like she said the other day."

"But now you're a counselor."

Kim nodded. "Yes."

"Do you miss teaching?"

"At times. I enjoyed being in the classroom, but counseling gives me even a greater sense of fulfillment." Stopping, she stared ahead, out over the mountains. "Teenagers are so unpredictable. My days are never the same. One minute I might be dealing with two freshmen squabbling over a misinterpreted conversation, the next with a senior crying over his grades, and then with a junior who I think is being abused by her boyfriend. Sometimes it gets even heavier than that."

Thad dropped his head against her shoulder and listened.

"There are days when I just want to sit down and cry because I know there is nothing that I can do to help."

Kim drew in a deep breath. She hadn't realized until just this minute how she needed to get away from school for a while. Her summer break was just too short; counselors usually work through most of the summer scheduling classes. She'd had little break.

"I imagine the kids can talk to you pretty easily."

She nodded. "But I can usually put their problems right back to them. Help them put things into perspective. Try to make them see where everyone involved is coming from. You know I do have that stubborn streak. My students know I'm there when they need a shoulder to cry on, but they also know I'll make them buck up and take the heat when they have to. They call me Sergeant Martin." She laughed. "Sometimes, though, all they want is a sympathetic ear. Whether they're having problems with parents or drugs or are pregnant, they all need someone to talk to. I think I'm almost a surrogate parent, at times."

"I'll bet you are."

Kim smiled and turned slightly. "There was this girl, one of my former students, who informed me at the end of this school year that she was pregnant. I've tried to help her as much as possible and now I'm afraid I've let her make me a crutch—something I shouldn't have done. She's called me all summer long. She'll probably be frantic that I'm not home yet."

"Did you tell her you were leaving?"

"Yes, but I was supposed to be home yesterday, remember?"

"Oh, that's right."

"Do you want to get somewhere to call?"

Kim shook her head. "No. She'll be fine. She has a mother who is trying hard to be there for her, and she must learn to depend on her a little more. She'll be okay. I'm sure of it."

"And what about you?"

She turned even more and studied Thad's face. "Me?"

Reaching out, he touched her nose and looked at her sympathetically. "You're worried about her, aren't you?"

"I worry about all my students, Thad."

"But you're worried about her more."

After a minute, she agreed. "Maybe. She's so young. Naive. I don't know what she's going to do with a baby."

Thad said nothing more for a while. Kim settled back against him. For the longest time, they let the warm afternoon breeze wash over them as she surveyed her surroundings.

But her thoughts returned to Melissa, the young pregnant student. Melissa had made a crutch of Kim, and she'd allowed it, but even worse than that, Kim had made a crutch out of Melissa. There had been too many Melissas over the years. The year before, it had been Christopher. Before that, Daniel and Ginny. Before that....

It dawned on Kim then that perhaps all these years she'd allowed her job to be the crutch. She'd gotten so involved in what she could do, give, and make better for all her students, that she hadn't given any thought to what she could do for herself.

Perhaps that's why none of the relationships she's had with men over the years had panned out.

Was she that determined to make her mother see that there was more to her than making some man a wonderful wife and having his babies?

Thad said something. She didn't hear. "I'm sorry, what did you say?" She pulled her gaze back to look him in the face.

"I said your job must be an extremely important part of your life, isn't it?"

She answered that it was before she'd really given it a second thought. Then in the silence that followed, she wondered if she'd made it important for all the wrong reasons.

Chapter Fourteen

T had brushed a tendril of wet hair away from Kim's face. Droplets of water clung to her lashes and the apples of her cheeks as her eyes sparkled up at him. In his arms, she felt like wet silk as their bodies glided together in the warm pool next to the waterfall. Her legs were wrapped around his waist and his arms held her close, her breasts crowded against his chest, soft, fluid, and sexy.

God, how he loved holding her. She made him feel primal and male and full of something he hadn't felt in quite some time. If ever.

Leaning in, he captured her lips in an urgent kiss. How he hated thinking about being separated from her. With Kim in his arms, everything felt...so right. Was she eager to return to that apartment, and her life before now?

"Have you ever thought about doing anything else?" he blurted out, wondering if he was thinking out loud. "I mean, what if someday, you couldn't find a counseling job? How important is that to you?" Thad knew that to win Kim's heart, he had to get to the middle of what Kim was, on the inside and out. Was counseling her life, just as ranching was his? He knew

jobs of her sort were few and far between in this sparsely popu-
lated area.

Her gaze narrowed as she contemplated his question. She
studied him for a minute, as if weighing her words very carefully. "Counseling and teaching are the only jobs I know how to
do." She paused and looked away, almost with an irritating look.
"Unless, of course, not counting if I got married and have kids
someday. I might make a halfway decent mother." Jerking her
gaze back to him, she continued, "Gee, that sounded so hokey.
What I mean is that I think I'd like being a wife and mother one
of these days, but I would never want to give up my job."

Thad felt like a boulder landed in his stomach. Kids? "So,
you'd like to have kids?"

She faced him again and nodded. "Someday. What about
you?"

"I'm too old to be a father."

Kim cocked her head sideways and tightened her grip
around his shoulders. A sly grin crossed her lips. "You're not
old, Thad Winchester."

"I'm forty."

"That's not old."

"How old are you?"

"Twenty-nine."

"Practically jailbait." Thad snickered. "But right now, you
make me feel pretty damned young."

Kim smiled back and held the connection between them.
He like her smile better than the puzzled look she gave him
earlier. "I think you'd make a pretty good daddy. You've lived
enough life to know what's important when raising a child. At
least that's my theory."

Leaning forward, Kim smiled and pressed her lips against
his. A swirling mist of desire rose within him. He urged his
hands lower into the water, smoothing them over Kim's firm

rear, forcing her closer against him. "I used to think I might," he whispered against her lips. "I just never found the right woman to be my child's mommy."

Kim pulled away and stared into his face. Her eyes searched, looking for something he didn't know if he could give. Slowly, he lifted her out of the water and carried her to the edge of the stream. Their clothes lay scattered, where they'd hastily left them moments before, so he laid her on the blanket of grass.

Lying beside her, he gathered her into his arms and held her against him. "Kim," he whispered. "You're making me crazy." Damn. What was he going to do without her?

She stroked his face. He relaxed his hold and let her lie back against the grass. With her head pillowed on his arm, she caressed while watching his eyes.

"Thad," she breathed, "I'm sorry. I shouldn't have mentioned children, and all that other stuff. I wasn't meaning to imply— I mean, I didn't...don't want you to think that I was pushing you into something—"

"Kim," Thad interrupted. It was now or never. They had to discuss their options. "We have to talk."

An expression lanced over her face that he wasn't quite sure how to read. "About what," she whispered.

"Where do we go from here, Kimmy?" he asks softly. "What happens when it's time for you to go home?"

She didn't answer him immediately, as if contemplating what her answer should be. "I have to go home, Thad," she whispered. "And from there, well, we'll just have to see."

He nodded and looked away.

How could she say that so quickly, without putting much thought to it? He didn't see. Never would. If she went home, he doubted he'd ever see her again.

* * *

A hazy orange glow shrouded the camp, dark except for the glow from the slowly dying ring of fire before them. They'd roasted hot-dogs for dinner, and then marshmallows later for dessert. The remaining smoke drifted in thin patches in the suddenly humid atmosphere.

"May rain tomorrow," Mack lazily offered to anyone caring to listen, or respond.

Jillie snuggled into Mack's side, her head resting against his chest, content as a kitten in her master's lap, Kim thought. Kim sat between Thad's knees, leaning back against him, his arms draped around her protectively. He didn't let her get too far away. Sometimes she wasn't quite sure what to make of his actions, but now she was too tired to contemplate any of it, and was only glad for his arms around her. The last marshmallow, crusty and lightly golden, drooped from the end of the thin branch she held in her hand.

"Want this one?" Arching her neck backwards to glimpse Thad's face, she lifted the stick high enough where Thad could reach out and grasp the end.

"I'm not sure if I could hold another one," Thad confessed.

Kim turned around and faced him. She watched as he slid the gooey mass off the stick, then tossed the latter into the fire. With his thumb and forefinger, he pinched off half the marshmallow and held it out.

She groaned, then opened her mouth. After Thad's fingers stuffed it in, she grasped his hand to lick off the last of the goo from his fingers. "You're killing me," she muttered through licks and small sucking sounds.

Thad groaned. "Uh-uh, I think it's the other way around."

Quickly, he stuffed the remainder of the marshmallow in his mouth and Kim watched as he licked his lips and fingers. Then moving onto her knees, she leaned forward and flicked away a tiny morsel from his mustache with her tongue, before planting a lingering kiss on his lips.

"Ah-hem, you two over there," Jillie shouted out. "The night's getting long, and we've got a day's ride in front of us tomorrow."

Kim turned into Thad's embrace and looked at Jillie. "So, what are you saying?"

"I think she's saying that we all need to turn in and get a good night's sleep," Thad offered. "And for once, she's right. Come on, Kim." He urged her to rise, and then followed her.

"Wait." Jillie and Mack rose as well. "You're right, of course, Thad, but before we do, Mack and I have something to tell you two."

Instinctively, Kim, knew that whatever it was Jillie was going to say, was going to change things. And she had half an idea what it was. Only, she hadn't expected it this soon.

Jillie stepped closer. "Kim, I know you think I'm impulsive and you've always tried to talk me out of my impulsive acts, but this time, I want you to hear me out before you say a word. Promise?"

Her pulse pounded in her ears. "Okay. Promise."

Jillie glanced from Thad to Kim and then to Mack. After a moment, she took a deep breath and continued. "We've been best friends for a long time, Kim. You got me through that first year of teaching. I don't think I would have made it without you. I really owe you a lot."

"You don't owe me anything, Jillie. You know that," she whispered. *Come on. Get it over with.* She felt Thad's hand grip her elbow from behind, which made her feel tense even more.

Jillie glanced again to Mack. "I don't really know how to say this other than just blurting it out. Mack and I are getting married."

She couldn't say she hadn't suspected it.

"Married." It wasn't a question.

Jillie hurriedly added, "...and I'm not going back to Kentucky. Well, maybe just for a few days to get my stuff and resign my job, but by then we'll be married."

Hells bells. "When?"

"As soon as we get back to Durango. We might want to get away for a week after we do. That is, if it's okay with you, Thad. Mack was going to talk to you." She directed her question to him.

Kim watched Thad glance from Mack to Jillie and then nod. Jillie was getting married? She wasn't going back to Kentucky? Thad's words interrupted her thoughts. "Mack you know that's fine...but have you two thought this thing through? Does she know all she needs to know?"

Mack stepped up to Thad. "It's all good, Thad. It's what we both want. We don't need any more time. We just need each other. I've waited for Jillie all my life and I'm not about to let her slip through my fingers now. I love her Thad, and she loves me. Anything else, we will handle."

Kim watched the intense stare that passed between Thad and Mack. There was something that both men were not saying

She turned to Jillie. "You're sure, Jill? This is so sudden. You and Mack don't really know each other that well. Things can change."

Jillie waved her off. "Damned sure."

"Then there's only one thing I can say." She stepped closer to her best friend and wreathed her arms around her neck. "Congratulations, you crazy girl," she whispered. Then after a moment, she turned and stepped back toward Thad, giving him awkward smile.

She really, truly, was happy for her. Truly.

Only one thing bothered her. Jillie and Mack had come to this conclusion so easily, so quickly. Why did it have to be so difficult for her and Thad? Or perhaps, she should say, for her? She'd seen the look that had crossed Thad's face earlier this afternoon when she'd told him, in no uncertain terms, that she was going back to Kentucky. It was as painful for him as it was for her.

A cold sliver of resentment crept up her backbone.

She was jealous of Jillie and Mack. Of the ease of their relationship. And she was jealous of their impending marriage, as well.

And quite frankly, she hated herself for it.

* * *

They broke camp just after sunrise and breakfast. The manties were all packed and tied, the mules loaded. And the horses were ready for their riders to lead the pack string further into the wilderness. To the west, dark clouds boiled on the far horizon. Kim watched Thad for a minute as his troubled face scrutinized the impending storm.

"Everyone have their rain slickers?"

"They're in the saddlebags. I checked," Mack replied. "Do you want to wait and see what's going to happen?"

Thad shook his head. "No. It's going to be a while. I think we can make it a couple of hours further. If it gets bad, there are plenty of places we can stop. To keep on schedule, we need to move."

Kim watched Thad's tired eyes as they darted back and forth from Mack, and then to her. The oddest feeling came over her, as though he were rushing, hurrying this thing on, so their relationship could come to a natural conclusion.

Ever since Jillie had announced about hers and Mack's wedding plans, Thad had seemed on edge. They'd made love quickly, almost fervently, after they'd retired to her tent. Then he had clung to her the rest of the night. So much so there were times she could barely move or breathe.

She wasn't sure what to make of it. Jillie's announcement had taken her a bit off guard, but she couldn't say it totally surprised her. Nothing Jillie said or did ever surprised her. Could it be that Mack's decision was the thing setting him off kilter?

Or was it something else entirely? Surely to goodness, Thad wasn't feeling pressure to ask her to marry him, was he?

At that realization, Kim stopped fiddling with her saddlebag and slid her gaze to Thad. Was that his problem? Was he contemplating the same thing?

Surely not. No.

And what if he asked her that? How in the world would she answer him?

She didn't know.

And obviously, he had no clue, either.

She watched Mack and Thad look over the camp one last time, checking the fire ring, making sure there were no permanent reminders of their visit. Jillie sidled up to her out of nowhere, beaming. Kim had to do an about-face with her thoughts.

"So, what's with you this morning?" Kim finally allowed herself to grin back. "Set the date yet?"

"Noooo," Jillie responded. "But it won't be long."

"Hm." Kim glanced toward Mack and Thad, now heading their way.

"Kim, are you okay with this, the wedding, I mean?"

Turning to her, Kim grasped Jillie's hand and smiled. "Jillie, I'm as happy as can be. I'm going to miss you something awful, but I want you to be happy."

Her friend beamed. "Really?"

"Really."

Jillie stepped forward and hugged her. Kim clasped her arms around her friend and hugged her right back. After a moment, they broke the embrace.

"I was just thinking about how all this is turning out," Jillie began again. "I mean, just a few days ago and you and Thad were at each other's throats. And now," Jillie elbowed Kim in the side, "well, I, for one, saw Thad sneaking into you tent late last night." She slowly nodded her head and widened her eyes.

"Gee, Jillie," Kim prompted, "I'd have thought you'd have better things to do in the middle of the night than spy on your best friend."

Jillie's jaw dropped. "I wasn't spying Kim Martin. I had to take a trip to the little girl's tree, and I just noticed the comings and goings of your tent!"

Kim rolled her eyes and sighed. This was hopeless. Jillie giggled.

Thad stepped up beside Kim and gently grasped her arm. "It's time we all get in the saddle and head up the trail, folks."

His expression worried her. More than before, when he was gruff and treating her like a small child, it bothered her. The whole tone of the light conversation she and Jillie had shared just seconds earlier had suddenly changed.

Something was wrong with Thad.

Jillie obviously noticed it as well. "Just a minute there, cowboy. Give me just one cotton-pickin' minute. Okay?" Jillie stepped in the center of the foursome. "I think, before we go on, that we need to establish just a couple of things here."

She eyed Thad directly.

"Go on."

"Would you not agree, Thad Winchester, that at the onset of this pack trip, you and Kim butted heads at every turn and were hell-bent on making each other's lives one living hell?"

Thad tossed Kim a quick glance. She saw one corner of his mouth turn up in a slight grin. "I would agree."

"Great." Jillie nodded and crossed her arms over her chest, then looked to Kim. "And would you not agree, Kim Martin, that at the very beginning of this pack trip, you wouldn't even have dreamed of making it with a cowboy?"

It was Kim's turn to grin. She caught Thad's eye. "I would agree."

Jillie's head dropped in a sharp nod. "Wonderful. And would you not both agree that for the past for a while now you've shared some meaningful times together and that things seem to be looking up for the two of you?"

Kim hesitantly glanced Thad's way again. His gaze caught hers. The grin was gone, replaced by a seriousness that Kim so easily recognized. "I would agree," she said softly.

Jillie turned to Thad. "And..." She gestured with her hands, trying to drag the words out of him.

"Yes," he relented.

Kim's heart jumped. Were things looking up for the two of them?

"Then why in the hell are you moping around like your best bull just died! I mean, you just admitted it. Things are going great between the two of you. It's only going to get better from now on."

Kim caught Thad's gaze and he smiled. Her soul warmed as she watched his face light up. Jillie was right. It could only get better from here. They'd figure something out, wouldn't they?

Thad stepped closer to Kim and Jillie walked toward Mack, linking her arm with his. "And to think, they only have me to thank. Right Mack? Oh, and you, too. Even if we had to lie and cheat and practically steal to get them together."

Kim couldn't speak. She could only look at Jillie. Realization slapped her in the face like an icy nor'easter.

They'd lied to him. Oh, God. All three of them. Why had that not occurred to her before now?

"A little deception here. A bit of trickery there. And before you know it, we've got a full-blown romance on our hands, Mack. Think we can get them to step up to the alter with us?"

Kim risked a glance at Thad. He could only stare at her, questioning. Thank God a hint of a smile was still on his face. First chance she got, she was telling him the truth. All of it. If she could only keep Jillie from running off at the mouth....

"It was hard getting those lawyers to cooperate at first, but you know those Ivy League men, always ready to jump on an extra buck. Now, of course, I can't take credit for those two grannies bailing out like that, but I wish I could. Sorry we had to lie to you, Thad, but it was the only way Mack and I could think of to get you to agree to this little adventure. And I so much wanted to experience the wild, wild west."

Shut up, Jillie. Kim silently prayed the words as she turned back to face Thad.

A myriad of emotions crossed his face. At first, she saw confusion. Then a ray of disbelief filtered through. Finally, his eyes narrowed as he stared blankly at her and his cheeks grew ruddy with anger.

He'd figured it out.

"What the hell is that supposed to mean?" Thad spit the words out of his mouth like foul venom, then turned on Jillie.

Jillie tossed a nervous glance toward Kim. "Oh, Thad, come off it. Just a figure of speech."

"I don't buy it." He directed his gaze toward Mack. "What did the three of you do?"

Jillie stepped in front of Mack. "Forget it, Thad. It was nothing. I was just making noise. You know how I am." Jillie's puzzled gaze caught Kim's.

"Tell him, Jillie." Stunned, Kim knew what they had to do

now. Jillie had to tell Thad the truth about this whole pack trip thing. Because if she didn't, he would eventually find out and he would never trust her again. "Tell him."

Mack stepped forward. "Thad, it was all in fun. Don't get your dander up."

The look on Thad's face frightened Kim. "Tell me what the hell you're talking about right now."

"Oh, all right." Jillie stepped up to Thad and parked herself square in front of him. "It's as simple as this. Mack and I met days before we took that trail ride up into the mountains, the one where Kim fell off her horse. That day, Mack told me about the two old ladies who had canceled their trip and so we finagled this plan so Kim and I could come, just so Mack and I could spend some more time together. We were hoping you and Kim would hit it off, but we really didn't think it would happen. You two are so totally opposite."

Jillie stared Thad down. Kim watched his face. It never cracked as he spoke. "Go on," he returned.

"That's it! You've got it all in a nutshell."

Mack stepped up beside Jillie. "Come on, Thad. We need to get started."

"No."

"But the storm's heading this way—"

"So those old ladies weren't your grandmothers?"

"Hell no," Jillie blurted out. "We don't even know them, isn't that a stitch?" She guffawed and then sucked in the laughter when Thad only glared back.

"Then you all lied."

"Sort of, Thad," Mack interjected, "but it was all in—"

"Actually, Kim was never really in on it, and she got duped about as much as—"

Thad swirled. "Where's the money from the trip?"

"Money?" Mack parroted.

Thad finally broke his stance and threw his hands into the air. Kim's gut wrenched. She didn't like what was happening. "Yes, dammit! The money! Where the hell is the money for the trip?"

Mack placed a calming hand on Thad's arm, which Thad promptly yanked away. "Thad, the two old ladies canceled weeks ago. I sent them a refund. I just didn't have the heart to tell you."

"What about the lawyers?"

"They were legit—until I bribed the arrogant one to come onto Kim, hoping it would spark something inside you. Then you nearly punched his lights out and I had to promise them both a refund since we cut their trip short. They were threatening to sue. Thad, look, I'm sorry to tell you this right now. I intended to as soon as we got back. There's no money."

Thad's face turned scarlet. There was a long, empty, silent moment before anyone uttered a word. Thad glanced from Mack, to Jillie, and to Kim. Then the only sound they heard was a gurgle of laughter that started deep in Thad's belly and rolled out of his throat in one giant guffaw.

Kim stared.

What was wrong with him?

Crouching down, Thad sat on a log, his shoulders shaking while he shook his head and continued to laugh. Then he looked straight at Mack. "There's no money?"

Mack shook his head. "No, Thad."

Thad wiped his eyes with the back of his hand. "That's perfect."

Kim was about to lose control. Had Thad gone nuts? "What's perfect, Thad?"

"There's no money," he returned, still huffing out a laugh now and then. "All these days I've been holding back, trying not to touch you, talk to you, kiss you. All because I've got some staunch notion that businessmen and their clients don't fool around." He snickered again. "All this week I've been driving myself crazy, you too, and if I'd known all along that Mack and Jillie had cooked up this scheme, and that there was no money involved, I would have—"

He stopped himself. Kim was glad. She wasn't too sure she wanted Jillie and Mack to know just exactly what he would have done had he known earlier that they weren't paying customers.

Standing, he drew closer to Kim and pulled her next to his beating heart. "I wouldn't have held off making love to you for so long," he whispered. His lips nuzzled the space just under her earlobe and Kim suddenly forgot that they had an audience behind them. She laced her arms around his neck and held him close. "I sorely regret that, Kim," he breathed next to her ear, "because our time together has grown so short, too damn quick. And I'm not sure I want it to end."

And at that moment, Kim didn't know if she wanted it too, either.

Chapter Fifteen

Thad took one look at the swollen river and silently swore. He'd expected the water to be up, but he hadn't expected it to be this high, or rushing this fast. Since they were now making their downward trek over the Continental Divide, they were at a point where rains high in the mountain over the past couple of days were now flowing downward and filling the streams at their level.

Ordinarily he wouldn't be concerned, he'd crossed with inexperienced riders before, but with Kim—he just wasn't sure if she could handle it.

Or maybe he was just being too protective.

He silently contemplated his dilemma. They could try wading in, angling the string up stream, but his gut reaction was that they were going to have to swim the horses across. If that were the case, then he'd just have to put Kim up next to him with his horse and let Sunshine cross with the pack mules. The mare was experienced enough. She'd know what to do.

"Want me to wade out and check the depth?" Mack's question jarred him. Thad glanced to his right. The women and the mules were still behind him.

Thad shook his head. "We've crossed here enough to know that we're going to have to swim. What worries me is that the river's moving at a fairly good clip."

"We'll be alright. Jillie can handle herself and Kim will do okay."

A bolt of panic settled in Thad's chest. "You think so?"

Mack grinned. "Sure. She'll do fine." Mack turned back to the string. Thad followed. He wasn't too sure Kim would be okay. He liked his plan better.

As he reached the three other horses and riders and the four mules, he once again stopped and perused the situation. Finally, Kim spoke.

"So, what's the plan, O Fearless Leader?"

The plan is to get us all back to the ranch in one piece. From there, he was going to do whatever he could to convince Kim to give their relationship some more time. Perhaps forever.

"The plan is this." He eyed all three of them, his gaze finally resting on Kim's face. "The river is a bit more swollen than I would like, but we've got to cross, and this is the best place, so this is what we'll do." He hesitated a minute, studying Kim's eager face. "Listen to me carefully. We wade the horse in until the water is thigh level, then slip off your horse and into the water. If the horse has to swim, then we'll swim alongside. Our bodies will act as additional leverage and help keep the horses afloat. You'll get wet, but it will be a safer crossing for both the horse and the rider. We can always change clothes after we cross."

He stopped and watched Kim's face. There wasn't a hint of concern there. He plunged ahead. "Kim, I want you to ride my horse, though. I'll lead us all in, then when you slip into the water, I'll be right there beside you. Sunshine has crossed a hundred times before and she'll be fine with the mules."

Kim's face drew up into a scowl. He ignored her and turned his horse toward the river.

"Wait a minute, Thad." He stopped and looked at her. "I don't understand why I'm riding your horse. Is there something wrong with Sunshine?"

"No, as I said, she's done this a hundred times."

"Oh, then there's something wrong with me, is that it? You don't think I can handle this, do you?"

It wasn't that. He simply wanted her close, to make sure she got across all right.

"Is this something you usually do with inexperienced riders, or just me? I want to know, Thad."

He huffed out a breath. "Kim, it's what I usually do for children. Most of the time adults can take care of themselves, but in this case—"

Her temper flared. "In this case, you feel I can't make it and you're treating me like a child?"

"That's not it, Kim."

She nudged her horse closer to his. "Then what is it?"

He lowered his voice. "Kim, I want nothing to happen to you, alright? Sometimes the horses get skittish. Sometimes their feet get tangled in the reins, or on a tree branch under the water. Sometimes it gets difficult to get across when the water's moving so quickly. I just want to make sure you're close by so I can help you if you get into trouble."

He could see in her eyes that she was not convinced. "But what about Jillie? Are you giving instructions for her to ride Mack's horse, to stay close to him?"

"Jillie has a mind of her own, Kim. She can do whatever she wants."

Her eyes widened. "And I have a mind of my own and I can do whatever I want."

"You'll do what I tell you to do." This was getting way out of hand. Couldn't she see he was only doing it for her own good? "The best place for you is next to me."

"The best place for me is where I choose to be. I'm crossing on Sunshine. I trust her. I'm going to do it by myself."

Panic gripped him. He had to talk her out of it. "Kim, you don't know the danger here."

She edged Sunshine closer. "I'll tell you what I don't know," she retorted. "I think I don't know you half as well as I thought I did. You don't trust me, you don't think I'm competent enough to do what you're asking the others to do, and you don't think I can make it in your world, do you Thad?"

Her words bit at him like an icy blast from the north. Was that what this was all about? Was he so fearful of losing her, of her not fitting in with his lifestyle, that he felt he had to coddle her, keep her safe within reach, should she decide that this life was too damned rough-and tumble for a lady like her?

Maybe so. But he'd be damned if he'd let her know that.

"Crossing a rain-swollen river is dangerous, even for someone like me who has done it many times. There are always unexpected problems to deal with, and someone like you, who hasn't been handling a horse very long, needs to be with someone who can make sure you cross safely."

"Bull!" You're making excuses, Thad. Admit it, you don't think I can do it."

It was true, he didn't. Maybe it was best to get it all out in the open. "No, Kim, I don't. I don't think you can make it. Across the river or in my world. It's a tough life. Hard work. And I'd have to coddle and pamper you every step of the way, just like now. It would never work. Face it, Kim. We'll never work."

Suddenly, he realized he was talking about a lot more than crossing the river. So was she. They were talking about their life together. And by the look on Kim's face, she knew it as well as him.

* * *

Kim swallowed the pain that constricted her throat. The piercing glint of his eyes made her nearly shiver. He was dismissing her like so much old shoe leather. In an act of indifference, she clenched her fists and braced herself on the mare. "I know why you're pushing this, Thad. You feel insecure about my leaving in a few days. That's it, isn't it?"

He scoffed at her words. Kim sensed his confusion. "I don't know what you're talking about."

"Yes, you do," she interjected. "If you push me away now, then you don't have to do it later. It doesn't hurt as much to say goodbye. Right?"

"Kim, that's not it."

"Then what is it?"

"I've already told you. I want you to be safe."

"You want to get me out of here because you're afraid that I can't handle myself."

He nodded. "Yes! Alright. That's it. I'm afraid you can't handle it, Kim. Dammit, yes, I'm afraid."

And I'm afraid I can't handle it when I leave you, either. Maybe it's better this way. "Well then, if that's the way you feel, there's no reason for me to hang around here any longer. I'll get out of your sight this very instant."

"Yeah, right." The look in his eyes defied her actions.

Ignoring the ache in her chest, Kim sat straighter in the saddle. She allowed herself one long, last look into Thad's face. "Point me toward Elk Park," she ordered, "and I'll be on my way. Then you don't have to be afraid, Thad, because I'll already be gone."

Thad didn't hesitate. He didn't even allow a flash of regret pass over his face. He didn't think she would do it. Well, she would prove him wrong. She would show him just how competent she could be, and that if she wanted to, she could make it in his world just fine.

He pointed. "Due west. Follow the sun. Can't miss it."

"Fine." Kim tightened her grip on the reins and heeled her horse in the flanks. Without thinking of the consequences, she urged the horse into a trot and headed due west, following the river. She didn't dare look back.

She thought she heard Jillie call out behind her, but the words faded away too quickly. A lot of junk was bouncing around inside her brain. And if she thought about it too much, she might just turn the horse around and make an utter idiot out of herself.

No chance. For once in her life, she was acting on impulse. And she'd damned well better make the most of it—or die trying. She had to show Thad that she could survive on her own if she put her mind to it.

* * *

Thad called himself every kind of fool for the past two hours. Why he'd wasted all that time thinking she'd come back, he'd never know. Why he'd insulted her, pushed her out of his life, he'd never understand either.

Where in the hell is she?

Initially, his gut reaction was that she would high-tail her shapely derriere right back to him within five minutes of leaving. Later, he'd expected her to come careening back at the first roll of thunder. Or at least at the first shaft of lightning to split the distant sky. Hell, he never expected she would head out alone.

But he'd been the idiot. A fool. How could he have treated her like that? All he wanted to do was protect her and he'd ended up treating her like a child. And she had reacted in the only way Kim would react.

Without thinking.

He wasn't dealing with some normal individual who did what was expected. He was dealing with Kim. He should have been ready for anything.

She meant what she said. She was going to make it to Elk Park. All by herself. Then she would head back to Kentucky— and out of his life.

And by God, she would probably make it. And they'd both be miserable for the rest of their days.

He'd been so frightened of losing her that he'd screwed up everything. And she'd had to prove her point. Prove to him that she could handle the wilderness. And worse, if he did find her, bring her back to the ranch, would she welcome his arrival? Or would it only confirm in her mind that he didn't trust her instincts. That he didn't think she could make it out here. Alone.

But the thought of her alone, out in this isolated wilderness, was the thing that spurred him on. He had to find her. She had no knowledge of the danger that might lie in wait for her. And he couldn't live with himself if he didn't try. If he found her and she was angry, then he'd suffer those consequences. He'd rather know she was safe and alive, than in trouble and he hadn't even tried to save her.

He'd rather risk losing her, than not go after her at all.

The storm had subsided an hour earlier—he hadn't picked up her trail yet. He knew the rain softened earth would easily reveal her horse's hoof prints if he stumbled upon her trail. It would be the only evidence he'd need to assure himself that he was traveling in the right direction. He prayed, silently, and then in half-coherent mumbles, while his keen eyes searched for any sign, any clue, that she had been this way before him.

Inside his chest, his heart felt as though someone had chopped it in two with a dull ax. The blood that the heavy organ forced through every vein and capillary of his body, burned with fear and remorse. How could he have said what he did?

How could he have told her he was afraid she couldn't hack it?

Thad jerked the horse to a stop and arched his weary back. It was a moot point. She would leave him now, he was certain, no matter how earnestly he apologized. He'd breached all trust, broken all ties, and if he did find her, he'd simply explain his shortcomings and admit he was a horse's ass, then he would see her to safety and head back to the ranch, where he'd sent Mack and Jillie hours before.

He was that sure the tables couldn't be turned back in their favor.

But there was no way he would leave her to struggle with the wilderness. There was no way he'd leave her out here, stranded. Even if she was a fool for darting away from them like she did. Thad knew deep in his heart that he'd forced her hand on the issue, and that whatever happened to her out there would all be on his shoulders.

His buckskin nickered, and Thad aimed his gaze at the ground. Immediately, he heaved a sigh of relief and silently thanked the powers that be. Crossing in front of him was a set of sloppy hoofprints in the mud.

A shiver of fear wrenched his soul. The hoof prints led directly into the river.

* * *

The cold seeped into Kim's bones like an icy specter. It was the first conscious feeling she'd felt for the past two hours or more. She wasn't sure exactly how long it had been since she'd rode away from Thad like an idiot.

She lifted her head to stare at her surroundings. Darkness and blowing water surrounded her from all sides. The storm had boiled up from the valley about thirty minutes earlier, darkening the sky and lending an eeriness to the mountainside. She'd stopped just long enough to search through the saddlebags to find the raincoat. After slipping it on, pulling the hood fully over her head and fastening out the damp and cold up to her neck, she'd arranged the long coat over her legs and horse's rump hoping that most of the water would run off and keep both her and the horse relatively dry.

It was pretty much a futile effort. The wind had picked up speed by then, blowing horizontal gusts of rain into her face and lifting the slicker away from her legs. But she'd kept the horse moving and before long, she peered through the sides of the hood and saw the edge of the forest in front of her.

Now, still on the horse's back, but under the protection of several large boughs of pine, she was certainly drier, but feared the lightning would start again, and she'd have to move from beneath the trees to find some other means of shelter.

She wasn't certain how long she'd sat there. The horse seemed in no particular hurry to leave, and if the truth be known, she didn't want to leave the protection of the trees either. So she sat as the slicing wind forced random rain drops through the pine needles, whipping them against her back and face and hands, and she cried.

She knew she could cry out in sobs and screams and no one would hear her. She knew, that if she wanted to, she could wail to her heart's content, but she also knew that none of that would do her any good. She'd gotten herself into this predicament, she was going to get herself out. And she really didn't want to cry, but the emotional upheaval her last few hours had provided seemed to warrant it.

So, she'd just let the tears silently fall down her face, mingling with the rain, her whimpering sobs swallowed by the rumble of distant thunder. And after a while, she felt much better. She still had no earthly idea where she was going, but she felt better.

When the storm finally passed, and rays of sunshine penetrated even the density of the forest, she decided it was time to trek on.

She figured that if anyone decided to follow her, she at least had somewhat of a jump on them, but she feared it wasn't enough. It was imperative that she see this thing to the end. By herself. If there was one thing she'd learned the past few days, it was that she could do a lot more than she thought she could. That she could set her mind to something and accomplish the task—and she didn't need Jillie to back her up. She could do it by herself.

And that was exactly what she was about to do. She was going to prove to Thad, Jillie, and anyone else out there who thought that Kim Martin was made of fluff, how wrong they really were.

Kim Martin was made up of a whole lot stronger stuff than that. And she'd prove it to them in spades.

But there was only one problem. First she had to cross the damned river.

She'd followed it for nearly an hour, not straying from its banks until she'd needed to seek shelter, so it wasn't long before she approached its edge again. Now, there was nothing to do but plunge in, trust her horse and her instincts, and pray.

Which is exactly what she did. In that order.

Sunshine faltered little but kept her head and lead Kim

directly into the rushing water. As the water rose, and she felt Sunshine becoming a little uneasy, she started to slip over her side, but not before she remembered Thad's warning about the horse's legs getting tangled in the reins. Quickly, she tied them close to the mare's body and gripped them with one hand while the other held onto the saddle horn.

Icy water splashed into her face and chilled her body as the horse moved confidently onward. Kim didn't take the time to think much about what she was doing, she just kept floating and paddling next to the horse, hoping she was still heading across river, and not down river.

The horse broke the rushing water, protecting her from its strength, and before she knew it, she felt rock river bottom and she and the horse walked up onto dry land.

At that moment, a feeling of exhilaration raced over her body and she hugged Sunshine's neck. Not that she wanted to prove Thad wrong. No, that wasn't it at all. It was that she wanted to prove herself right. If anything good came out of this entire trip, it would be that she could go home knowing that she had given this pack trip thing everything she had in her.

For miles, Kim allowed the mare to pick her way casually over the terrain as they dodged a few more small showers. She hoped that at least the horse had some sense about what direction they were heading. Had she traveled this way before? Could she help Kim find her way to Elk Park by rote, much as the trail horses could?

Kim decided she couldn't be sure, as much as she trusted old Sunshine, so she was going to have to watch for signs that might help her point the mare in the right direction home.

The mountains had a fresh-washed feel about them. The

storm had raced over the mountains and down the other side, leaving only brief remnants of rain as a reminder. Stopping Sunshine, Kim shoved the hood off her head and glanced behind her, then all around, as she contemplated where they might be.

Behind her the mountains seemed to ascend, the sky still dark. Turning forward again, she realized she was on a downward trek. Quickly, she glanced about her. To her far right, she saw a stream flowing downward. The Continental Divide. They had obviously crossed over it and now she was heading west! Hopefully, toward Elk Park.

A small thrill zinged up within her and she allowed a hint of a grin to form on her lips.

"All right." She murmured the words to the horse, as much as herself. "What else did Thad tell me the other day?"

A glimmer of hope gave her strength. "The Colorado Trail," she stated matter-of-factly. "All I have to do is keep the sun in front of me and search for the trail. It should lead me straight into Elk Park."

Kim smiled. With a lot more gumption than she'd had an hour earlier, she urged the horse forward, keeping her eyes open for any sign of the trail that would lead her out of here. It might just be her only ticket home.

Chapter Sixteen

There were waterfalls all around her. Kim delighted in the trickling sound and the sparkling diamond droplets bouncing off solid rock. The creek was in front of her, and all around her, at the same time. Smiling, she slid off her horse, and with the reins held loosely in her hands, walked the mare closer to the water's edge so she could drink.

The horse drank, and Kim dug her canteen out of the saddlebag. After taking a healthy drink herself, she slipped the canteen back into position and removed and folded the now dry rain slicker, placing it as well back in the saddlebag. After she did that, she breathed deep of the crisp, clean air and gazed at the spectacular beauty of the mountains.

After the storm had left, she'd found herself immersed in the scenery, savoring the clean, pristine beauty of the mountains. For the first time, she really was in no hurry to get back to Kentucky. The Colorado mountains fascinated her, but the thought of returning to her home threw a dismal curtain over the landscape.

Funny how Thad had insinuated himself into her life so quickly. He'd fought it and so had she, but it felt like they'd shared a lifetime together. Of course, there was always the underlying current about her leaving at the trip's end. But that was all water under the bridge now.

Now, all she had to think about was getting out of here and back to her students in a couple of weeks, and her Junior League meetings, and her bi-weekly manicures. Of course, there was shopping at the mall. And an occasional dinner out with friends. Not to mention her Mother's Sunday-after-church dinners.

Kim closed her eyes. How had her life become so mundane? So superficial? So...fake?

Shaking herself out of those thoughts, she perused the western sky. The sun was dropping rapidly in front of her. Rays of orange and pink shot up into the dusk. The trees glistened like deep green emeralds. The streams and waterfalls rushed by at an exhilarating pace. The evening was crisp and alive and calling to her. Speaking to her in such a manner that she almost felt she could talk back, and that Mother Nature would understand.

"This is not superficial, or mundane, or fake," she whispered, searching her surroundings. "This is real." A small rabbit scurried from beneath some low brush, startling Kim, and she jumped, then laughed. "I am real. I feel more alive right now than I've ever felt."

Blowing out a cleansing sigh, she stood contemplating those thoughts, not sure to what end they would conclude. She only knew that when she left here, she would miss this place—and that likely, her life at home needed an upgrade.

Kim moved toward the horse. Since the storm had left, the evening sky was free of clouds, but the air had turned decidedly cooler. Her clothing was still a bit damp, and she wished for a heavier jacket or a sweatshirt. If all else failed, she'd slip back into the rain slicker, knowing it would protect her somewhat from the chill.

The day's end held her spellbound. If it weren't for the fact that she knew she had to make camp somewhere soon, she would have liked to have parked herself on a rock amidst the waterfalls and simply watched the sun slip over the horizon. But she couldn't. She had to find shelter somewhere. She'd waited too long.

Slipping her foot again into the stirrup, she raised her body into the saddle and turned the horse away from the water's edge. After urging her up the small rise she'd moments earlier descended, she glanced at a pile of rocks to her right. Funny, she hadn't noticed them before. As she moved the horse closer, an odd sensation crept up her neck and tripped down her spine. The rocks were piled high on top of one another like a miniature henge.

A rock cairn! A Colorado Trial marker?

Excited, she let her gaze mark a path leading into the forest, and her heart picked up its cadence. She'd found the Colorado Trail! And it was heading west. Hopefully, she was only hours from Elk Park.

But there was no way she could travel much further tonight. Her immediate concern was shelter. And the only way she could do that, was to follow the trail into the forest and hope that she would find someplace, anyplace, where she felt safe enough to lay her bedroll for the night.

And as she headed down the trail, she realized she was not afraid. She was in control. And she was enjoying the beautiful, peaceful wilderness that surrounded her. Perhaps she should be afraid, but after her initial shock wore off about what she'd so impulsively done, and after crossing the river, the fear had left her. Replacing the fear was a sort of self-reliance that she'd never in her life felt before.

And it felt wonderful.

The only thing that marred her otherwise pleasant thoughts

was the way she and Thad had parted. She would have liked for it to have been different, but she guessed that wasn't to be. If he could only think of her as someone to share his life with, not protect from life, then maybe they could have worked things out. But if he viewed her as someone he had to coddle, then it would never work.

She had to make it to the train. And she had to do it by herself. That just might be the only redeeming feature of this entire trip. And it would be the thing she'd take home with her and remember for as long as she lived. That and her memories of loving Thad, however bittersweet.

Heck, she might even tell her grandchildren about it some-day. Well, most of it, anyway. If she ever had grandchildren.

Within thirty minutes, the forest was too dark for her to continue. The narrow path wound its way through a host of trees, and she'd searched for even a small clearing where she and the horse could rest, but it seemed there wasn't anything.

She rode on. The horse gingerly picked her way through the dark. Their pace was slow, and Kim knew that before long, they needed to stop. Any further along the trail and she wouldn't be able to see five feet in front of her, and she couldn't risk the horse slipping and tumbling off a trail that led to nowhere.

Finally, a break in the trees happened, and she tiredly urged the horse to the right. Stepping from beneath the umbrella of forest to beneath the night sky, she noticed a few stars sprinkled overhead, a full moon, and a shaft of light over the clearing. Unsure exactly what she should do, she dismounted and, by moonlight, untied the bedroll from behind the saddle. She led the horse to the edge of the clearing and tied the reins to a low-hanging branch.

A hoot went up from the tree above her and Kim froze. Standing still for another minute, she waited, but the sound didn't come again, and Kim decided that the least of her worries was an old hoot owl asserting authority over his territory. In the back of her mind, though, there were other concerns she harbored about sleeping out under the stars. Minor worries, like snakes and rodents, and bigger ones like elk and bear. She hoped that by staying close to the horse, the mare would warn her of any approaching danger. She just hoped she wouldn't trample her in her sleep to flee that danger.

Maybe she should sleep on the horse. Do people do that?

Regardless, she had to get through the night.

Kim removed the large rain slicker from the saddlebag and laid it over the ground first, its outer repellent side next to the ground. She hoped the coat would help keep ground moisture from seeping into her sleeping bag and ward off a chill. Then, she laid the bedroll on top of that. She searched the saddle-bags for anything else that might be useful, but only came up with a pair of binoculars, which she thought might come in handy tomorrow, and a half-eaten granola bar left from her lunch. She'd eaten the sandwich and apple and the other half of the granola bar throughout the earlier part of the day. She contemplated saving the bar for breakfast but reasoned that her body needed fuel to keep her warm throughout the night, and that perhaps tomorrow, she'd arrive at the Elk Park spur early enough in the day so she could buy something for lunch there.

She could only hope.

The mare nickered and tossed back her head. Kim froze beside the horse, straining her ears. Had she heard something? Sensed, smelled something?

Silence fell about her makeshift camp. Night birds twittered above her in the trees and in the distance, she heard a faint howl. Unmoving, she allowed only her gaze to shift across the small clearing, trying to spy any movement that seemed out of the ordinary. Her ears were alert to any sound that might warrant danger. If need be, she was ready to snatch up her bedroll and slicker and mount the horse again quickly.

But after a moment, the horse settled back into grazing mode and Kim relaxed. With granola bar in hand, she settled deep into the sleeping bag, zipping the thing up nearly to her ears.

With a sigh, she felt the tension slide off her shoulders, and her eyelids grow heavy. As nervous as she was about sleeping out in the open, she was just as tired. And when the moment came that, she thought she might drift off to sleep, the mare lifted her head again and sounded a warning nicker.

And another one answered her from down the trail.

Another horse! People?

But the moment's elation was stifled in the next second when panic set like a rock in her abdomen. What kind of person might travel on a horse out in this wilderness at this time of night? Would it be someone she could trust? Heaven knows she was vulnerable to just about anything. She was totally at the mercy of whomever was out there.

Her horse neighed again, and the other echoed. Louder. Closer.

Kim bolted upright in the sleeping bag and pulled it close under her chin. Suddenly, she was shivering. Another neigh. Another echo.

"Kim!"

His voice stunned her. Thad? For a brief eternity, she contemplated him finding her and all that it meant. He was ruining everything. She had to do this alone. Should she answer him? Or should she just let him go on and pass her by?

Again, the horses called to each other.

"Kim!" His voice sounded frantic. "Are you out there?"

She hesitated only a second more.

"Over here, Thad," she returned tentatively. There was no

use letting him wander around in the dark, endangering both himself and his horse.

They broke the clearing and Kim could see the buckskin in the moonlight. She stood up. "Where are you?" he called out.

Relenting, she answered. "Over here."

Within seconds, he and his horse were standing directly in front of her. Quickly, he dismounted.

She didn't give him a chance to speak first. "What are you doing here?" she hissed, still harboring a bit of resentment.

"Trying to save your hide. That was an asinine stunt you pulled."

"It wasn't a stunt, Thad. And I'm doing quite fine, so you can just go right on back from where you came."

"Oh, no you don't. I'm staying."

Kim smiled in disgust. "Here we are again. You making demands and expecting I obey. Haven't you got it yet, Thad? I'm a woman of my own means. I make my own decisions."

It was dark, but she could still make out the steel hardness of his eyes. "And I can make it to Elk Park. It shouldn't be much further."

"You're right. It's not far. And I'll see you there safely tomorrow if that's what you want, but tonight, I'm staying here with you." He shifted toward the horse. "I've got a tent, and I don't mind sharing."

I'll bet you don't.

Kim didn't want to share. "I'm fine where I am. This is a free country. Set your damn tent up anywhere you please."

"And you're going to share it with me."

"I like sleeping under the stars."

"Since when?"

She contemplated that question. "Since..." Embarrassed and angry that she'd brought up the thought of them sleeping together under the stars, she turned and plopped back down into her sleeping bag on the ground.

She felt Thad's gaze upon her. Laying there, she realized her heart was beating way too rapidly and that her breathing was coming in short, shallow gulps. Damn him! He was ruining everything!

Thad whirled away from Kim. Alternately relieved at finding her, and angry at her refusal of his help, he hastily untied the bedroll from his horse's rump and tossed it to the ground. Within a matter of a few minutes, he'd tied his buckskin close to Kim's mare and had pitched the tent and rolled his own bedroll out inside. Throwing one last glance toward her, he gave it one more shot.

"Kim, the tent will keep off the chill and dew. You'll be sick before you know it, lying on the ground. I don't think you can afford to be sick for Jillie and Mack's wedding, do you?"

He stared at her still form. When she didn't answer, he lifted the flap of the tent. Before entering, he tossed out one more thought. "I promise, I'll not bother you. I'll not touch you or talk to you, but please, get in the tent."

She still didn't answer. Reluctantly, Thad entered and left the flap half open. After kicking off his boots, he slid into his own sleeping bag and faced the wall of the tent. But he knew there would be no sleeping for him tonight. He couldn't possibly sleep with her out there like that.

He turned to call out one more time. "Kim, please..."

"All right, Thad. You win. This time." She flipped back the tent flap and tossed her bag inside. Turning, she zipped the opening closed and arranged her sleeping bag against the opposite wall. He watched her slip inside, her back turned to him. After a moment, he listened as she sighed heavily. He let his own tired body fall into the bag's warmth, but his eyes never left her back.

"I'm a horse's ass, you know," he told her a bit later, his voice barely above a whisper. "I'm the reason you took off like that. I feel responsible. That's why I came."

Her back didn't move, and he had no way of knowing if she was awake, or asleep. If she heard anything he said.

"Actually, you were right. I am afraid of what's going to happen at Elk Park. If I pushed you away before then, then I wouldn't have to face the inevitable. I was stupid. I didn't mean all those things I said to you, Kim."

He paused and waited for any sign that she heard him, but there was none.

"If I said I was wrong, and that I was sorry, would it make any difference? Would there be any way, any chance..." Thad huffed out a breath and flipped onto his back. Hell, this was useless. He'd blown it, all of it. There was no way she would consider coming back to him, and he knew it. His lifestyle was all wrong. He was too rough around the edges for a woman like her. And she had her life all laid out before her—back in Kentucky. It was unfair of him even to ask. So, he wouldn't.

Turning onto his side, he clamped his eyes tight against any thought, or scene, or memory that dared cross his vision. It was going to be a restless night.

When Kim heard Thad's breathing finally slow, she quietly turned over to look at him. He'd turned his back to her as well. She couldn't blame him. He'd poured his heart out in so many words, and she'd simply lain there, and didn't respond. Ignoring him.

He had ruined everything. She had so wanted to do this by herself. To make it to Elk Park so she could, at the very least, feel like she'd accomplished more on this trip than becoming Thad Winchester's lover. So she could then feel free to love him, knowing that she could make it in his world. Then he wouldn't have to pamper and coddle her for the rest of their days.

Because she couldn't stand for him to think of her lacking. For him, she wanted to be a strong woman. One who he wouldn't have to make alternative arrangements for when it came to crossing the swollen rivers of life.

She had ignored him. Let him believe she didn't care.

There were two things she couldn't ignore now, and those were the bitter tears flowing down her cheeks, and the constricting pain she felt in her heart. But when it came right down to it, if he'd said the words she really wanted to hear, that he loved her and he wanted her to stay forever, that they could work things out, how would she have reacted then?

Would she be willing to give up life as she knew it, for Thad?

* * *

Warmth rushed over Kim's face in soft currents. Sleep wafted through her and held her in its embrace like thick hot fudge, delicious and satisfying. She woke slowly, her brain gently rousing and becoming aware of the heavenly warmth wrapped around her body, as well as the crisp coolness that nipped at her nose.

Vague remembrances of where she was and why she was there nagged at the fringes of her understanding. There was something important she had to do today. Something that involved...going home.

She attempted to roll onto her back, but there was a strange heaviness draped over her side. Confused, and still a bit disoriented from her drug-like sleep, she squirmed beneath the covers, trying to free herself from their binding.

Her eyes fluttered, and bits of light pierced the morning haze. Again, she tried opening them, and when she did, only then came fully aware of her situation. She was in Thad's arms, staring at a row of buttons on a soft flannel shirt, and a V of curly chest hair.

The heaviness of his arm drew her closer, and again, she felt the warmth of his breathing against her face, inhaled the deep, raw male scent of him. Instantly, she decided she could react in one of two ways. She could toss his arm off her and push him away, or she could savor the moment just a bit longer, pretending she was asleep.

"Good morning."

She pushed away. The choice was taken from her. He was awake and watching her.

"Morning." Rising, she cautiously and hesitantly turned away from him and began rolling up her bedroll. "What time is it? Do you know?" She avoided looking into his face.

"Are you in a hurry?"

You might say that. "What do you think?"

"It appears that you are."

"Well, you're right."

"Can't you even look at me, Kim?"

It took all the self-control she possessed not to scurry out of the tent at that moment. But she didn't. Slowly, she lifted her face to look at Thad.

He was lying on his side, propped on one elbow. His shirt was open several buttons down and she glimpsed a small expanse of his firm chest. Her gaze traveled to his chin, his thin lips, and then to his eyes. Sleep softened, they looked almost pleadingly sad. Her heart ached. A tingle of remorse shot up within her. She wanted more than anything to go to this man and fall into his arms. But it would do her no good. There could never be anything permanent for the two of them.

But could it hurt to have something temporary? Just this last time?

Thad's gaze met hers and held. Kim swallowed and wet her parched lips. She didn't know what to say or do. And she knew if she stayed there like that, for one moment longer, the tears would come, and it would be all over.

"I have to leave, Thad," she whispered. "I have to." She needed time. And she had to go home to think it all through.

He nodded, hesitantly. Reluctantly? "Then I'll take you to the train."

* * *

The Elk Park spur of the Narrow Gauge Railroad loomed before them. Kim stared at the coal-burning locomotive, which made daily trips from Silverton to Durango. She wondered how many cowboys had dropped their women off here in the past, because the delicate creatures were more suited to the refinement of the east, than the rough living of the west. Certainly, she wasn't the first. And she probably wouldn't be the last. The irony of it all set her a bit on edge.

Heaving in a thorough sigh, Kim glanced at Thad, then dismounted the horse. All morning long her thoughts had returned to one notion. What would she do if Thad asked her to stay? Even if just for a little while? Could she forget the silliness of the past few days and try a normal existence with him?

But he would not do that. All morning long, he'd sat sternly in the saddle on the horse in front of her and led her down the mountain and into Elk Park. He hadn't asked her then. He wouldn't ask her now.

Somehow, she was disappointed.

She rounded Sunshine and looked up into Thad's blank face. "I guess you'll take the horse back with you?"

He nodded, and she handed him the reins.

"How long will it take you to get back to the ranch?"

"Depends," he answered blandly.

"On what?"

"On whether I take the direct route or decide to hang around up there a while. I've got no reason to hurry home."

Kim bit her lip. "Oh." Glancing back at the train, the hikers and tourists hurriedly boarding, Kim figured she'd better get moving as well. "I think I need to go now."

She watched as Thad reached into his back pocket for his wallet and slipped out a thin piece of paper. He shoved it at her. "Here's your ticket. It's part of the pack trip package."

Hesitantly, Kim took the ticket while engaging his gaze. "But I didn't pay for the trip. Do you want me to pay you?"

He grimaced and shook his head. Maybe it would have been easier if they'd kept it strictly business, she thought. "I don't want your money, Kim."

Then what do you want? The words were almost out of her mouth, but she stopped them. It was no use. "All right." Dropping her hand to her side, she glanced back at the train. Slowly, she returned her gaze to Thad. "I have to go."

He dropped his head. "I know."

"I'll call when I get home."

"Whatever you want. I don't know when I'll be there."

She backed up a few steps. "Oh. Well, I'll try again if I don't get you. Or you can try me."

But she knew both scenarios were unlikely to happen.

She backed away a couple of steps from Thad and his horse. Passengers boarded behind her. It was difficult to tear her gaze away from his. Then his lips moved.

"Kim, if I asked you to stay... If I told you I loved you, would it make a difference?"

Something difficult to describe surged up inside her and tightened in her chest. Her breathing grew shallow. Her eyes never left his. "Are you going to tell me you love me? Ask me to stay?" she whispered.

Thad glanced off then, and Kim watched him stare into the mountains. Train sounds grew louder behind them and people rushed by. Neither of them noticed.

Finally, Thad faced her and said, "No, I will not ask you to stay."

Kim tried to show little emotion. It was difficult. Her heart was pounding too damned erratically. "Then I guess it wouldn't make a difference, would it?"

He shook his head. Their eyes held the longest connection, then without saying good-bye, Kim turned and walked away, unable to endure his blank gaze a moment longer. As she approached the train, she blindly made her way through the crowd and merged into the sea of people ascending the steps to the train. She never looked back.

She couldn't bear to see him standing there, all alone.

Just one thought reverberated through her head, her heart. He hadn't said he didn't love her, only that he would not ask her to stay.

There was a difference.

* * *

Thad stared at the railroad tracks until the tail end of the train was lost into the horizon. His chest ached. His gut hurt. He refused to let go of the tears that burned his eyes. Kim was gone. He'd let her go. And she'd never be back. He was sure of it.

If only she'd asked him for more time. If only she'd given

him some reason to ask her to stay, he would have risked it. But she hadn't. And he didn't possess the stamina right now to go out on a limb and get burned. He just couldn't do it.

He tied the mare's reins to his saddle and pivoted toward the mountains. He had a two day's ride in front of him if he pushed it. Three if he took it easy. Getting back to the ranch wasn't a priority. When he'd told Kim earlier that there was nothing to go home to, he was right. And he wasn't sure why he'd even mentioned it. It was just the truth.

He didn't resent the fact that she'd left, he simply regretted that he didn't have the guts to ask her to stay. To figure out a way for them to make it. To tell her he'd call her. No, they were both better off just letting it go right now. Before they'd become too attached, too much in love.

Feeling rather distant, he headed back up into the mountains, where he belonged.

Chapter Seventeen

For the ten-thousandth time, Kim stared down at the newspaper in her lap and attempted to read the front page. It was useless. For the ten-thousandth time, her brain refused to comprehend what she was reading.

Jillie punched her shoulder. "Coffee?"

She shook her head. "No. I'll float out of here if I drink anymore."

"How about some toast, then. You look a little pale. Maybe you should eat something, instead of drinking all that coffee."

Kim knew she was probably right. But coffee was the only thing that seemed to get her up and going these days. For the first time in eight years, she was having difficulty dragging her butt out of bed and getting to school. Thank goodness for Jillie. She had managed to work miracles with her for the past month.

But she figured Jillie wasn't doing it out of any sense of loyalty. Jillie was fighting her own battle right now and keeping herself busy was her best defense. Kim had simply reduced herself to a mass of human, blubbering flesh.

"Better get a move on, we're going to be late again. You

know how Len Harper loves to tattle to the front office whenever any of the faculty is late."

Kim rose from her seat and tossed the unread paper aside. Yeah, she knew. "Len Harper needs to retire," she returned blandly. "Give me ten minutes."

"Sure. We've got the time. Just no more than ten, you hear me?" Jillie called up the stairs of their townhouse apartment as Kim headed for her bedroom.

She didn't know why she had no energy. Ever since they'd returned from Colorado, she'd had difficulty getting herself up and off to school. Jillie kept telling her she was in mourning for Thad.

Ridiculous, she'd bantered back. She'd mourn for no man. She dressed quickly and made a quick attempt at makeup, then met Jillie at the front door.

"If you don't mind me saying so, Kim, you could use a refresher course on makeup application." She reached out and smoothed a finger along her cheek. "This isn't like you. You have foundation caked against your ear, and mascara dotting your upper eyelid. If you will not pay any more attention than that, then perhaps you should just skip the makeup altogether."

Kim thought it sounded like a good idea. One less hassle in the morning. She shrugged her shoulders. "It's a thought."

Jillie drove and Kim watched the scenery. After a while, Jillie broke the Golden Rule. The one they'd agreed on about never talking about Colorado.

"Do you ever think about Thad, Kim? I mean, you know, when you least expect it, does his face ever pop into your head?"

Like every night when I lay down to go to sleep, she wanted to say. "Jillie, we're not supposed to talk about that."

"I know, Kim, but we're going to have to talk about it at some point. It's been over a month and ever since we vowed we wouldn't mention it again, it's been eating at me. And I know it has been you, too."

Kim stared at her. "What makes you say that?"

"Because you look like hell, you've lost about ten pounds, and you cry into your pillow every night."

"I do not!"

"Yes, you do!"

Kim turned away in disgust. "Well, at least I don't moan Thad's name in my sleep, like you do Mack's."

Jillie sighed. "You do that, too, only I wasn't going to mention it."

Kim snorted. Silence filled the space between them in the small sports car.

"You know," Jillie began again, "sometimes I wonder if I was wrong, walking out on Mack like that."

Kim continued to stare out the window. "You had no choice, Jillie. He was mean to you that last day."

"Not really, he was just...confused, I think."

"Phft. He was mean, Jillie. And rude. He pushed you away with no real explanation. You were planning to get married, for God's sake!"

"I know and I've been thinking about that. There was something he wasn't tell me. I'm just not sure what it was."

Kim shook her head. "I wish we both had something concrete to go on. Those men...can they not express feelings? Say what they want and need? I don't get it."

"I don't think we behaved any better," Jillie said.

"What do you mean?"

"Well, Kim, when Mack was trying to break up with me, I pretty much told him to go fuck himself."

Kim's brows raised and she stared at Jillie. "Oh?"

"Yes."

She thought about that for a moment. "And I, on the other hand, simply left. I just turned around and left."

"You had good reason to do what you did."

She turned and looked at her. "Oh, yeah. I got upset because all he wanted to do was protect me. To help me. I had to go all ballistic on him."

"It was the principle of the thing, Kim."

She knew it was. "If he had just wanted to talk about it. If I hadn't gone and flown off the handle. If both of us hadn't been so damned stubborn. Sometimes I wonder..."

The car slowed as Jillie pulled into the school parking lot. They heard the early bell ring as they both exited the car and headed into the school.

"Sometimes you wonder what, Kim?"

She shook off the thought. "Never mind."

Jillie walked silently beside her. "Hey, maybe we should order in pizza tonight, rent a couple of sappy movies, and cry all night long. Maybe then we'd get it out of our systems."

Kim shook her head. "I promised Mom and Dad I'd have dinner with them tonight. Then I've got a League meeting."

"Forget the meeting, we'll do the movies."

Kim looked at her, horrified. "I can't miss a League meeting, Jillie."

"You could if you wanted."

"But I've never—"

"Then perhaps you should."

The second bell sounded. The one that told the kids to head to homeroom. They were late again.

"Geez," Kim moaned, "Eagle-eye Harper is watching. We'll be on the list for the next few days. Better watch your P's and Q's."

Kim scurried off, leaving Jillie to face Len Harper. She wasn't in the mood to discuss any further what she sometimes wondered about. She was at work now, and her students depended on her to have a clear head.

Even if that was a near-impossible feat to attain these days.

* * *

Thad watched the Narrow Gauge pull away from the station at Elk Park for the last time this season. He'd thought that in time, it would get easier. He was wrong. Every time he watched that puff of steam chug into the mountains, he thought of Kim.

Of her leaving him in this very spot, and him doing nothing to stop her. If only he'd been thinking straight. If only he'd thought to convince her to stay, just a little longer, so they could think about what they were doing. Make a plan. It might have worked.

His chest drew tight. He'd also thought that by now he would be over her. Again, he was wrong. He didn't know if he would ever be over her.

"Well, that's finished until next summer," Mack offered as they both stared at the disappearing train.

"Yup."

"Now you've got the time to do what you need to do. So why don't you go for it?"

Slowly, Thad rotated his gaze toward Mack. "And what is it I need to do?"

"Go get her."

"You're so quick to give advice. Why don't you do the same?"

"Because it's too late for us. I screwed that up royally. But you—I think you can patch things up in a heartbeat."

Thad shook his head. "I wish I was as optimistic."

Mack studied Thad's face. "If I thought I had half a chance with Jillie, I'd be out of here on the first plane in the morning,

Thad. But I don't. I permanently screwed that up. Besides, I've got too many other problems to deal with now. But you, that's a whole different set of circumstances. There's nothing keeping you from going to Kim."

"Only the fact that we live two time-zones apart and that one of us would have to give up an entire lifestyle if we stayed together."

"And that would be a tough decision?"

"I don't think she would be happy here."

"Would you be happy there, with her?"

Thad contemplated the question. "Sometimes I think it wouldn't matter where I was, as long as I was with her."

Glancing away, Thad thought about his own words. Would he be happy anywhere if he had Kim? Would he be willing to give up the ranch, the life he'd always known, for her?

"If I had Jillie back," Mack added quietly, "I think I'd probably live on the moon, if that's what she wanted."

Thad knew Mack was missing Jillie something awful. He also knew that Mack's problems had intensified ten-fold since Jillie had left. Mack's personal life was a bit complicated, and Thad could understand him not having the strength to deal with getting Jillie back right now. But Mack was wrong if he thought there was nothing keeping him from going to Kim. There was everything keeping him away.

"She said she would call when she got home. She didn't. I think that sends a pretty loud message."

"Thad, we've been over this a hundred times. You both are pig-headed fools, waiting for the other one to make a first move. You're either going to have to take the risk or wallow in your own self-pity for the rest of your life. You can do something about this situation now, or you can stay miserable. Believe me, if I could alter what I've done, I would. Why don't you, for once, take the bull by the horns and make a damned decision about this."

Thad pulled his gaze away from Mack's face and perused the empty landscape in front of him.

"I never took you for a quitter."

The words stung, and Thad swung his gaze back to look at Mack. "I'm not."

The pack season was over for the year. The last train out had taken the handful of hikers and tourists back to Durango. His cattle were already moved closer to the ranch. The barren mountains in front of him reflected the empty longing in his heart. And all that loomed in front of him for the next few months was a cold, empty ranch house on a cold, lonely mountain.

Unless, like Mack said, he took the bull by the horns.

* * *

"Mom, for the last time, I'm not interested in dating Susan Elder's son. I know she's your best friend from college and you've explained many times that he's a successful stockbroker who just moved into the area, but I have to repeat, I'm not interested!"

Kim set her iced tea glass on the table with a little more force than she attended. A lone ice cube jumped up and splashed across her mother's linen tablecloth.

"Kimberly!" her mother exclaimed. "There's no need to take that tone with me."

Kim closed her eyes and pinched the bridge of her nose. For weeks now, it seemed a tiny, nagging headache always lay just behind her eyelids. Lack of sleep, she guessed. Maybe stress. She wasn't sure exactly what to attribute it to.

She opened her eyes and glanced across the table. Both her parents were staring back at her.

"Something happened to you on that trip to Colorado, didn't it, Kimberly? Do you want to talk about it?" Her mother's urgent expression bothered her. Kim glanced to her father's expectant gaze.

"Nothing happened to me in Colorado," she whispered. *Except that I fell in love.* "I've just been under a lot of stress at school. I'm sorry, I didn't mean to take it out on the both of you."

"You're not yourself, Kim," her father lamented. She searched his face, her gaze settling on the depth of his knowledgeable eyes. "Something's bothering you. I hope that whatever it is, you will work it out. You realize we're here for you."

Kim sighed and glanced at the table. "I know that, Dad."

"Kim," he began again after a minute, "your mother and I need to talk to you about something else. Are you up to listening? It's important."

A moment of panic settled around Kim's heart. "Is everything okay?"

"Everything's fine."

"Then what's so important?"

Her father embraced her mother's gaze with a smile, then he turned back to look at her. "I'm retiring at the end of the month. We've bought a house in Florida."

Kim sat in shock. "When did this all come about?"

"About a month ago. When you were in Colorado. We've been thinking about it for some time. You just seemed so preoccupied. We wanted to wait a bit, until we finalized the plans, to tell you."

"And now they are?"

"Yes," her mother answered. "We haven't decided what to do with the house here in Kentucky yet. We could keep it if you wanted to live in it, but we would charge you rent and you'd take care of the utilities, of course."

Kim sat back in her chair. "Wow. I don't know. I mean, of course. That would be great. But... Can I have a moment to process this?"

Her mother smiled and patted her hand. "Of course, darling. There is time."

"When are you planning to move?"

"We'll be in our new house for Christmas."

* * *

Catherine Hellman's voice droned on and on in Kim's ear. The first order of business was the charity auction. Second on the agenda was the League's contribution to the new hospital wing. Then she went on even more about what kind of pasta salad to serve at the horse show luncheon. Katie McIntyre didn't think they should have anything with black olives, since so many people were allergic to them. Caroline DeVries liked black olives. Should we have lavender napkins, or spice it up with something bold, like neon green? Catherine queried the group.

Kim didn't care if the napkins were pink with chartreuse polka-dots.

Then came the committee reports. Brette Bonner reported on the state of their treasury. Kirsten Vanlandingham reported on the invitations to the horse show. Cally Cooper lamented that the silver trophy trays they'd always used were discontinued by the trophy shop and she had no idea where to look to find a replica.

Kim huffed out a long, thorough breath. Who gives a flying leap?

Her entire life was in the toilet, she'd given up the only man she'd ever loved, nothing was going right at school, her parents were moving to Florida, and all these women could discuss was the color of napkins and whether to put black olives in the pasta salad? Give me a break! Doesn't it ever get any deeper than this?

Someone called out her name.

"I'm sorry, what?"

"Your committee report, Kim," Catherine replied with a hint of disgust. "For the charity auction. How many businesses have you contacted and which ones have you committed?"

Kim stood slowly, her committee report in hand, and glanced around the room from woman to woman. These people were barely acquaintances. She didn't owe them diddly-squat. She owed herself a whole lot more.

She tossed her report on the lap of the woman sitting next to her. "The committee reports," Kim began, throwing back her shoulders just a little squarer, "that the committee has nothing to report. And as of this moment, I officially resign from the League."

* * *

Melissa Potter sat crying in the principal's office. Her mother sat opposite her with the coldest look on her face that Kim had ever seen on a woman. Brady Johnson, the principal, sat behind his desk, a scowl over his face. And Kim crumbled and uncrumbled the wad of paper in her hands repeatedly and tried to hold back the tears, herself.

"I'm tellin' ya there's no use in this girl goin' to school anymore," Melissa's mother chided. "I need her at home and she's gonna be big before long anyway, and what good's it gonna do her to get a few more months of school in when she's gonna have to quit after the baby gets here anyway."

Brady Johnson cleared his throat. "Mrs. Potter—"

"It's not Mrs. Potter, not anymore. Just call me Carol."

"Carol," Kim interjected, "Melissa is a brilliant student. She wants to go to school. Isn't there some way we can work this out? I've contacted some local day care centers and one of them will let Melissa's baby stay all day for free if Melissa will volunteer to work there for half of her school day."

"We don't take no charity."

"It's not charity, Mrs., uh, Carol. She would work off what she owes them. Melissa only needs a few credits to graduate. We'd work it out here at school and could even provide her transportation to the center. Won't you please reconsider?"

There was a momentary silence. Kim glanced at Melissa, who was throwing her a look of thanks from her watery eyes.

Melissa's mother stood and headed for the door. "I thank you for your time, but Melissa and I have a lot to do at home. I've got three others younger than her, one still in diapers. Melissa's sixteen, she's young, maybe later she can get her GED, or something."

Kim stood, desperation aching in her heart for Melissa, whose eyes flashed in desperation back to her. "But Mrs. Potter. Please. Melissa needs an education to do right for the baby."

Carol Potter swirled. "Melissa's gotta do right by me. She made her bed and had her fun. Now she's got to lie in it. Ain't no worryin' about it, it's done and over with. Ain't no different than what I had to do myself. Now, we're leaving. Melissa, get your things."

As the pair walked out of the principal's office, Melissa's tear-filled face glanced back at Kim as she mouthed the words, "Thank you." It was all Kim could do to hold back the tears. She waited a full thirty seconds, then gave Brady Johnson a goodbye wave and headed for her office.

Thankfully, it was after school hours and the halls were clear. Just a handful of kids were milling about the gym. Ball practice, her mind registered.

She pushed open the door to her office just as the tears filled her eyes. With blurred vision, she quickly entered the small room and briskly shut the door behind her, pushing in the lock on the doorknob simultaneously. With her back against the door, she finally let the sobs overcome her.

Bittersweet tears trailed down her face. For Melissa. For her parents. For Thad. Oh, God. For Thad.

Sucking in a cleansing breath, Kim pushed a palm over her eyes to rid them of tears and stared at an unusual mass of color on her desk.

Her heart jumped.

Scarlet primrose, lavender columbine, and bright red Indian Paintbrush wildflowers were bunched together in a beautiful crystal vase, centered in the middle of her messy desk. Kim gasped, then reached out to touch a tender petal. Did she dare hope?

"You do not know what I had to go through to get those here." His voice came mellow and tentative from the corner of her office. Startled, Kim glanced to where Thad rose from a chair she kept there, looking ridiculously out of place with his Wranglers and Tony Lama's and his Black Resistol.

Oh, but you look so damn fine, Thaddeas Winchester.

"They're beautiful," she sniffed. *You're beautiful,* she wanted to say.

"Looks like you've had a bad day."

He strolled across the room and traced a trail of tears on her cheek with his forefinger. Kim peered into the pools of his eyes and felt her tears begin again.

"I've had a bad month," she whispered.

"Seems to be going around," he replied, studying her face. "I've missed you."

Kim sighed deeply and smiled, her eyes never leaving his. "I've missed you like crazy." His finger still traced her cheek.

"What are we going to do about it?"

Kim knew exactly what she wanted to do. She'd known it for a long time, she guessed, but needed to come back home to realize that a well-grounded life was nothing if the one you loved wasn't in it.

"I want to go home," she breathed.

He pulled back and cocked his head slightly. "To your home?"

She shook her head. "No. Things here are changing and I'm really not sure this is where I belong anymore. But I want a home. And I want it with you, Thad."

Thad bent closer and placed his lips gently, breathlessly, across hers. "Kim," he murmured, "I want to be wherever you are. I don't care where home is. You tell me what you want. I'll give up everything if I have to. I just want us to be together."

She finished the kiss while lacing her arms around Thad's neck. He encircled her with his arms. "Home, Thad Winchester, is wherever you are." She smiled. "Wherever we are together. But I have to tell you, I'm missing those mountains somethin' awful."

Drawing back to look at her, Thad grinned. "Really?"

She nodded. "Really."

"But there may not be teaching jobs there."

She shrugged. "Then I'll teach our kids."

"Kids?" he laughed. "You want kids, too?"

"And ponies."

"Horses."

"Whatever." She pulled him close and placed a long, passionate kiss on his lips. "Will you teach them to ride?"

"Uh-uh," he returned. "You will."

"Me?"

"You can do it. With a little practice."

She stared into his face and smiled. It was going to be all

right. Everything was going to be all right. "I can't wait to get back to the mountains."

He pulled back and cocked a brow at her. "It's been a sad situation around there lately between Mack and me. Sure you can handle it?"

"Do we need to bring Jillie with us?"

Thad thought about that a moment. "Naw. Let them figure out their own damn lives. All I want at this moment is to settle in on yours and mine." He nuzzled her neck and whispered, "I can't wait to take you home with me. Are you sure?"

Grinning slyly, and holding him tighter, she returned, "Cowboy, I've never been more certain of anything in my entire life."

* * *

Thanks for reading!
Want to read Jillie and Mack's story next?
Scroll on for Chapter 1 of The Cowboy's Secret Baby.

Chapter One–The Cowboy's
Secret Baby

August

"I don't understand."

Behind her, Jillie Abernathy heard the early morning rustlings of the trail camp. Horses nickered. Utensils banged against pots and pans in the makeshift kitchen. The low voices of wranglers peppered the early morning as they prepared for their last day of the pack trip, punctuated by the muffled sounds of tents collapsing and guests chattering while helping pack the mules. Wind whistling through a stand of nearby Colorado mountain pines provided a steady backdrop to the conversation she'd been having with cowboy Mack Montgomery.

This had been her life for days. Now, it was over.

All of it. Over.

She looked hard at the tall, lean wrangler standing in front of her. He'd been a dream come true—had fulfilled her every cowboy fantasy, and more. She'd had him for two weeks, and had fallen hopelessly, and unexpectedly, in love. Since Mack hadn't responded, she repeated her words. "Mack, I don't understand."

It was a statement, but it was really a question. The question mark trailed off in her brain, even though she tried to sound firm and matter of fact.

Inside she was dying.

This isn't happening.

Mack searched her face. She watched his gaze flick back and forth unsteadily over her features and land on her eyes, shift to her mouth, and then back to her eyes again as if he really didn't want to stare—yet couldn't drag his gaze away.

"I know you don't, Jillie. But let's face it—these past two weeks were great. Real great. Lots of fun. Now it's time to move on. You have to get back to Kentucky and I have to get back to work."

Lots of fun. Shit.

She tilted her chin. "I know that."

"So, you do understand."

In disbelief, she shook her head. "Not really. I don't understand at all, Mack." *What does he think I am? Some silly schoolgirl planning to ride off into the sunset on those big pack horses behind us and live happily-ever-after in the mountains?*

Well, that thought had crossed her mind. Hadn't it? They had talked of marriage.

"I guess you are going to have to explain it to me," she said. If he thought she was going to make it easy for him, he could think again.

He glared. "We need some time apart. You get that we can't have a relationship, right? The distance and all, and well...."

"There are these things called phones, Mack. And email. And texting. Even damn snail mail letters if you prefer. And guess what? Airplanes. And cars. There are ways to do a long-distance relationship."

"Neither of us have the time or energy for that, Jillie. We're busy people."

"If we make it a priority, we can do it."

The staring again. "Of course. If one wanted to go that route."

Jillie couldn't believe what she was hearing. "So, the bottom line is you don't want to go that route."

He nodded. "That's right. I don't."

"What are you *really* saying, Mack?"

"I'm saying it ends here. I'm not the kind to get attached, Jillie. This few days... They were a mistake. I don't want to be joined at the hip with any woman."

She laughed. "Just say it. You're not the marrying kind."

He bristled.

She paused. Hell, she'd said the *M* word. Then she added for good measure. "Mack, if you think it's too soon to get married, I get that. It's okay. We were rushing things. But let's give it some time. That's only fair."

His face turned stoic. Obviously, he didn't think that was funny. "I'm not the marrying kind, Jillie. I enjoy being unencumbered."

"Big word for a cowboy." The words were out of her mouth before she knew it.

He put up a hand. "Don't, Jillie."

"You're just the screwing kind then?"

He narrowed his gaze. "It wasn't like that and you know it."

"Then how was it? It sure meant more to me than a casual vacation fling."

"But that's just what it was, Jillie. And it ends now."

"And when did you decide this? Before or after we had wild monkey sex earlier this morning? Or did you know this all along?" Suddenly, she was nauseous. Hell, the last thing she wanted to do right now was puke.

"Don't go there either, Jillie."

Queasiness hit her stomach like a cannonball. *Crap.* "Then

this is it?"

He glared hard, and then looked at his boots. Shuffled his feet. Glanced to his right. Then, back to her face. "Yes. This is it."

Every bit of air pushed out of her lungs. Now she was light-headed. "Like, goodbye? We'll never see each other again? Have a great life?"

He nodded. "If you want to put it that way, yes."

She didn't want to put it that way.

"Why?" The word squeaked out smaller and weaker than she would have liked. She felt like yelling. Wanted to yell at him. All sorts of words flew around inside her head. Words like *liar*, and *bastard*, and *lying bastard sonofabitch*. But only one little word fell off her lips. "Why?"

"I told you why. It's for the best. For you. For me. Look, just head back home to Kentucky and your students, and I'll bet you'll find someone new to be with before football season starts."

Jillie scowled. Her life back in Kentucky had nothing to do with this. She could feel her face screwing up into a ball, and imagined the result wasn't very pretty. "I don't want someone else and I don't even *like* football."

"Just a metaphor. Or whatever," he said.

"More big words from the cowboy. I'm impressed. I thought I was the English teacher." That was another low blow and she knew it.

He ignored her. "We had a great time, though, didn't we?"

A great time. She fought the sting of tears. "Peachy."

Jillie crossed her arms, stepped back, and looked over the cowboy she'd spent every night cuddled up with in his sleeping bag. Riding beside him over the mountains. Working alongside him when they made camp. And yeah, the sleeping bag part....

"Just what I was after," she muttered. *What a fool I have*

been. Then she said louder, "I thought we had something special. Different."

He shifted again and peered off behind her shoulder.

She added, "You told me you loved me. You asked me to marry you."

He closed his eyes briefly. Mack stepped back a few steps and shoved his hands into his pockets. "Jillie, look. You're a great woman. It's easy to get caught up in things here in the mountains, away from home. I know you have this thing for cowboys, but you know how it is—you'll go back home, reminisce about how you got your fantasy lover, and I'll be old news before the week is out. You'll be on to some other guy."

His words wounded her to the pit of her gut. Fantasy lover? "What in the world do you think I am? I'm appalled you would think such a thing of me!" Her stomach hurt, and she rubbed her abdomen.

He shifted. "Face it, Jillie. I was on your bucket list, right? It happens all the time with girls from back east. They want to fuck a cowboy so they can go back and brag to their girlfriends."

"Oh my God!" She bristled and squared her shoulders, then rushed toward him to stab a forefinger into his chest. "I did not! I never thought such a thing about you!"

Laughing and standing firm, he countered, "Oh sure. I heard you and Kim talking. Cowboy lust, right? You were telling her you had it. You were aching to have a cowboy. Well, you had one. Now it is over. Besides, you live in Kentucky. I live in Colorado...."

"This is ridiculous."

He shrugged. "You know I was using you too, right? Move on, Jillie."

He was using me? "You are an ass."

"Yes, I am."

"You weren't like this a week ago. Hell, or yesterday. You

were a gentleman. You said and did the right things. You were happy to be with me—you even told me you loved me—and now you are telling me you think all I wanted was a cowboy conquest, and that you were using me to get off? What the hell, Mack? Where are your cowboy code scruples?"

He didn't immediately respond—just stood there, stoic, unmoving. "Like you said, I'm an ass."

She whirled and took a few steps away, then turned back to glare at him. "Yes, you are. And you are still avoiding my question. Twice now."

"I didn't hear a question."

She cocked her head and crossed her arms. "True. It wasn't a question. It was a statement. You told me you loved me. So, listen closely because here is the question—was that was a lie?"

He retreated a step.

"Look. It's the last day of the trip," he said. "I'll be busy and won't be able to talk to you when we get back to the ranch, so...."

"So, this is goodbye." *And you don't love me. Liar!*

Jillie jerked her chin up again. How many times am I going to make him freaking say it?

His lips thinned out and finally, his eyes stopped shifting. He looked straight at her. "Yes. Goodbye, Jillie. Safe travels home." He turned and began walking toward his horse.

"Go screw yourself."

Mack pulled up short, paused, and then walked on. Jillie watched him move farther away, a lump in her throat the size of Durango. Why was this happening?

He didn't look back. And she promised herself she wouldn't, either.

* * *

Get *The Cowboy's Secret Baby* today!

About Maddie James

Maddie James is the bestselling author fifty-plus romance novels and novellas published worldwide in seven languages. Available in ebook, trade paperback and audio, her titles span the romance genre from contemporary to suspense to paranormal romance.

Affaire de Coeur says, "James shows a special talent for traditional romance," and *RT Book Reviews* claims, "James deftly combines romance and suspense, so hop on for an exhilarating ride."

Learn more at www.maddiejames.org.